SPANISH ART SONG
IN THE
SEVENTEENTH CENTURY

RECENT RESEARCHES IN THE MUSIC OF THE BAROQUE ERA

Robert L. Marshall, general editor

A-R Editions, Inc., publishes six quarterly series—

Recent Researches in the Music of the Middle Ages and Early Renaissance
Margaret Bent, general editor

Recent Researches in the Music of the Renaissance
James Haar, general editor

Recent Researches in the Music of the Baroque Era
Robert L. Marshall, general editor

Recent Researches in the Music of the Classical Era
Eugene K. Wolf, general editor

Recent Researches in the Music of the Nineteenth and Early Twentieth Centuries
Rufus Hallmark, general editor

Recent Researches in American Music
H. Wiley Hitchcock, general editor—

which make public music that is being brought to light
in the course of current musicological research.

Each volume in the *Recent Researches* is devoted
to works by a single composer or to a single genre of composition,
chosen because of its potential interest to scholars and performers,
and prepared for publication according to the standards that govern
the making of all reliable historical editions.

Subscribers to this series, as well as patrons of subscribing institutions,
are invited to apply for information about the "Copyright-Sharing Policy"
of A-R Editions, Inc., under which the contents of this volume
may be reproduced free of charge for study or performance.

Correspondence should be addressed:

A-R EDITIONS, INC.
315 West Gorham Street
Madison, Wisconsin 53703

RECENT RESEARCHES IN THE MUSIC OF THE BAROQUE ERA • VOLUME XLIX

SPANISH ART SONG
IN THE
SEVENTEENTH CENTURY

Edited by John H. Baron

Translations and Text Commentary by Daniel L. Heiple

A-R EDITIONS, INC. • MADISON

To
Jamie Heiple,
Bernice Judith Baron,
and
Miriam Singer Baron

Library of Congress Cataloging in Publication Data
Main entry under title:

Spanish art song in the seventeenth century.

(Recent researches in the music of the baroque era,
ISSN 0484–0828 ; v. 49)
Spanish words also printed as texts with English
translations: p.
Includes biographical references and index.
1. Songs, Spanish—17th century.   I. Baron, John H.
II. Heiple, Daniel L.   III. Series.
M2.R238   vol. 49   M1495   84–760432
ISBN 0–89579–203–6

Contents

Preface

Introduction

The beauties of Spanish solo art song of the seventeenth century have been almost completely forgotten for nearly three centuries. During the seventeenth century itself, however, the Hispanic contribution to the solo song repertory was acknowledged throughout Europe and the Americas. Politically, Spaniards controlled large regions of the two hemispheres, and wherever Spanish administrators, *conquistadores*, and settlers went, so did their art songs. Moreover, Italian, French, Dutch, German, and English professional and amateur musicians sang and imitated Spanish art songs.

The cause for the neglect of such a historically and aesthetically important repertory is easy to determine. Nearly all *tonos humanos* and semi-sacred *villancicos* were preserved only in manuscript. The best copies were in the Royal Palace in Madrid and in the nearby theater in the Buen Retiro Park, and both of these repositories were destroyed by fire in the seventeenth and eighteenth centuries. The remaining exemplars of these songs are scattered in large and small archives (where only some works have been catalogued) in such distant places as provincial Spain, England, New York, Italy, Mexico, Guatemala, and much of South America.

Modern scholars have discovered only a few of these songs, a smaller number of which have reappeared in relatively modern editions. The first such edition, by Felipe Pedrell, is limited: only part of the text of any one piece is given (never more than one or two *coplas*, or strophes) and now, eighty years later, it is a rare and hard-to-find, though still useful, volume.[1] Miguel Querol has published two excellent collections in recent years: *Cantatas y canciones para voz solista e instrumentos (1640–1760)* (Barcelona, 1973) and *Tonos humanos del siglo XVII* (Madrid, 1977). The earlier Querol collection is representative of early eighteenth-century, rather than seventeenth-century, solo art song, whereas the later one contains sixteen songs from the second half of the seventeenth century. Two small collections with a total of seven songs were edited by Graciano Tarragó in the 1960s.[2] The present anthology, then, is the first sizeable printed collection of seventeenth-century Spanish solo art song devoted exclusively to that repertory, containing songs from the entire century. Each song is included here in its entirety with complete texts, and this edition draws on many newly discovered examples.

The songs, most of which are for soprano or tenor, are presented here in modern notation, with modernized text and realized basso continuo, so that singers will be able to perform them easily. The Critical Commentary will enable scholars to reconstruct the source for each piece, though significant editorial changes in the songs are enclosed within square brackets in the music. Complete English translations of the Spanish texts are also provided.

Historical Perspective

The songs in this anthology, which appear here in approximately chronological order, were apparently written for aristocratic audiences either at the royal court, theater, and convents in Madrid or at the various city palaces, theaters, convents, and country estates of the nobles. At least one piece (by Aranies; no. 4 in the present edition) was written for the Spanish occupation community in Italy. Insofar as they are court songs, these pieces are similar to contemporary, printed French airs. In seventeenth-century France, the Parisian court songs were either of the more sophisticated *air de cour* genre, based on pastoral poems of the highest literary order, or of the more mundane, squarer *chansons pour boire et danser* genre, based on lesser poems that were often somewhat inane. In Spain, there were similar subdivisions early in the century. Some of these Spanish songs, such as the one (no. 5) transcribed here from Luis de Briceño's *Metodo* (1626), are dance songs (*pasacalles* and *folías*), with folk-like texts and ritornellos that are purely instrumental dances; other songs, such as the one by Aranies (no. 4) and those transcribed from Ballard's 1609 and 1614 *Airs de cour* volumes (nos. 1–3, which are in practically all respects typical serious French airs), are musically and poetically more subtle.

Also in the seventeenth century there was the distinction between sacred and secular art song. As far as we can tell from the indications on seventeenth-century manuscripts, *tono*, *tono humano*, *solo humano*, and *tonada* were used synonymously and usually referred to a secular song, while the term *villancico* always indicated a sacred or semi-sacred composition. However, seventeenth-century usage is not always exact, and therefore it is not surprising to see "tonada" sometimes used for sacred pieces. The sacred *villancico*, often with texts that seem to be secular but that have religious symbolism, is contrasted with the secular *tono humano* or *solo humano*, often related to or borrowed from theatrical music (just as the French airs were often taken from dramatic *ballets de cour*). Despite the terminological and textual distinctions, the musical styles of *villancicos* (which evolved from secular song) and *tonos humanos* are quite similar, and both consist of *estribillos* (refrains) alternating with *coplas* (strophes). This close relationship between sacred and secular art song is comparable to that in seventeenth-century Germany, where, however, the solo *Lied* was basically a middle-class genre, not an aristocratic one. In Germany, too, there were relatively unsophisticated dance and drinking songs, as well as the more ambitious, artistic *Lieder*, which were sometimes pastoral and sometimes moralistic. In Spain the stylistic similarity between the *villancico* and the *tono humano* is reflected in the works of many composers who flourished between 1640 and 1680, such as José Marín, Juan Hidalgo, Cristobal Galán, and Juan del Vado.[3]

By the last decade of the century, there was a new dichotomy in Spanish art song: this was between the traditional *tonos humanos*, cast in *estribillo/coplas* format, and new Italianate *cantadas humanas* that alternated recitatives and arias. Sebastián Durón is credited with having introduced the Italian type to Spain. Because examples of his *cantadas* are found in the collection of Palencia's cathedral, where he worked from 1686 to 1691, Durón's introduction of the *cantada* may be dated ca. 1690. Some of his *cantadas*, as well as some of his more traditional songs, appear in this edition (nos. 23–26) for the first time in modern transcription. We also present some of Juan de Lima Serqueira's songs as evidence of the transition from the *tonos humanos* form to that of the *cantadas humanas*, including the hybrid *cantada* "O corazón amante" (no. 30), which includes both the recitative-aria format and an *estribillo*. Indeed, the introduction of Italian forms and styles into Spanish music was met by a storm of protest that lasted well into the eighteenth century.[4] Defenders of the "true" Spanish style, a style evident in most of the songs in this collection, objected to the increased emphasis on fancy vocalizing and the freer harmony and voice-leading of foreign music. The controversy was never fully resolved. Consequently, throughout the eighteenth century and later both the more traditional Spanish style (as represented by the *tono*) and the fashionable international style (as represented by songs based on cantatas, opera arias, and settings of romantic texts) were cultivated side by side.

The Poetry

Almost all the poems set in the songs in this collection have the form of the seventeenth-century *villancico*, which is not a metrically fixed form.[5] It consists of a refrain, a series of stanzas, and the return of the refrain, sometimes after each stanza, sometimes after only the last stanza. This form evolved from the sixteenth-century courtly practice of writing verses or stanzas (*coplas*) to accompany short two-to-four-line poems, often of popular extraction and irregular versification, that functioned as refrains (*estribillos*). Thus, the songs, which are usually the unique sources of these texts, have an AB . . . A form, with the musical theme and poetic structure of the A-section (*estribillo*) often being popular in nature. These short, popular, mostly anonymous poems have been appreciated from the sixteenth century onwards for their simplicity, delicacy, and vitality.

The poems in this collection employ a wide variety of metrical forms, from the irregularity of the traditional *villancico*, as in no. 6, to the sophisticated versification of no. 21. Most of the *coplas*, in those songs that have them, employ the traditional *romance* (ballad) or *romancillo* (a shorter line of *romance*) meter and rhyme scheme. Number 21 uncharacteristically uses the antiquated *arte mayor* (a line of four amphibrachic feet, popular in the fifteenth century), which is perfect for a $\frac{6}{8}$ dance rhythm. Number 7 relies on the rhythm of words with an antepenultimate accent, most of which are learned neologisms. The poem is quite artificial in its structure and, characteristic of such a *tour de force*, somewhat vague in its meaning.

Most poems in this collection can be classified as amorous or religious; but the range of ideas within these categories is quite broad, and the fact that nearly all the poems deal with love, either profane or divine, makes such a division less significant. The secular songs were probably written for plays or court entertainments, whereas the religious *villancicos* and *cantadas* were written for performances in church on high feast days.

Stylistically, some of the poems have a definitely popular air, such as the light *estribillos* of nos. 12 and 13, the traditional eye-imagery in the text of no. 1, and the subject matter of the love of the dark lady in no. 2. Others are high baroque, such as no. 19 with its complicated imagery of love as war. Although such imagery is traditional, in this poem it is so complex that it consistutes a novelty. Other aspects of high baroque are seen in the nearly unintelligible obliqueness and the mythological references of no. 21, the pomp and grandeur of the imagery used to describe the dawn in no. 14, and the delightful play of wit and language in no. 22.

Many of the poems depend on the conventionalized language and psychology of unrequited love. Numbers 9 and 10 praise the suffering that love must endure. Number 24 is based on the traditional concepts of love: the silent suffering of the lover and his suppressed desire to express his love. But the play on ideas is so subtle as to almost escape meaning. Number 27 takes delight in the fact that the haughty and disdainful woman must fall in love and, like the man, suffer the pangs of love. Number 11 tells a love story, relying solely on nature imagery. Number 29 argues for the naturalness of love, showing how it is a part of nature. Number 2 wittily plays on the love of a dark lady, an image familiar to readers of English poetry from Shakespeare's sonnets. Similar are the texts of nos. 13 and 15, which are light, almost comic descriptions of love. Number 12 is satirical, nearly bawdy, in its ridicule of the lascivious woman and her permissive husband.

The text set by Briceño in no. 5 is poetically the most interesting in the anthology. The literary tone of the text suggests that it is a collection of separate and distinct songs brought together and revised by Briceño. The second stanza is known in other sixteenth- and seventeenth-century sources as well as in modern oral tradition. The first two stanzas are fine examples of traditional lyrics and demonstrate the typical elusiveness of imagery in this type of poetry.[6] These lyrics make a simple statement, often about some natural phenomenon, and the image is applied to a new and often erotic context. The interpretations are based on certain norms established by the body of poetry itself or on the reader's imagination. When taken literally, the poem says nothing of love;

however, the prevailing poetic conventions enabled the reader to infer a deeper meaning from the nature of the imagery. For example, in the first stanza (see Critical Commentary, Texts, and Translations), the little dove and the green tree suggest youth and vitality, and the brush of wings and leaves suggests a physical contact, a playing with love. Thus, the allusive, suggestive nature of these first two stanzas is itself the chief poetic quality. The last two stanzas seem to be learned imitations and lack the subtle suggestiveness of the purely traditional verses. This could be said of most of the refrains (estribillos) in this collection, with the possible exception of nos. 11, 12, and 13, which could be traditional. Numbers 6, 20, 23, and especially no. 10, just to point out a few, are clearly composed for the song at hand, and, while they show little of the delicacy of the traditional lyric, they are full of baroque elegance and love of play.

Not only do the sacred and secular pieces often have the same musical and poetic form, but they often resemble each other in their language. This is because the sacred villancico employs the amorous imagery of the mystical poets, based on the tradition of the Song of Songs.[7] The attempt to express divine love in the strongest terms of profane love was a constant of the Middle Ages and Renaissance, although in some respects it culminated in the poetry of the Counter-Reformation, where poets unabashedly used the tenderest endearments to express their love of God and Christ. Numbers 6, 20, and 26 are good examples of this kind of expression. Number 8 relies on the amorous image of the courts of love. Number 16, on the other hand, sounds religious because it addresses the beloved as "my . . . master," but that convention comes from the troubadour imagery and is secular. Some of the religious texts are simply pious, as no. 25, while others are exhortatory, such as no. 23, which is a straightforward appeal to reason for reform and conversion.

The Music

Basically these songs are set syllabically, although there are occasional short, expressive melismas. In the estribillos there is often repetition of whole poetic verses, as well as repetition of individual words, with corresponding musical repetition; but in the coplas, verse repetition (if it occurs at all) usually affects only the final poetic line. Only no. 9 uses repetitive syllables (ce-ce, que-que, ta-ta); however, the repeated "ay" as a sigh, which occurs in this song, is commonplace in the repertory as a whole.

Musical form generally follows that of the text, though in some songs there are extra repetitions determined by the composer on musical grounds (e.g., in nos. 1, 3, and 4). There is also word-painting in these settings (e.g., on "alegres" [= happy] in three of the five coplas of no. 1; and on "suspiráis" [= you sigh] in no. 23). However, typically baroque violation of accepted Renaissance voice-leading for the sake of expression occurs only rarely in the tonos (e.g., the diminished fourths in no. 20). In the cantadas, however, use of such baroque voice-leading is a part of the pervading Italian influence.

Most of these works are in ₵3 or 3 meter, transcribed here as $\frac{6}{8}$, with the triple subdivision (1–2–3; 4–5–6) predominating. Syncopation and hemiolas, characteristics of seventeenth-century Spanish vocal music in general, are found in many of these solo songs (e.g., nos. 1, 11, and 12). The songs are tonal but largely limited to triads and dominant sevenths with root progressions by fifths and fourths; however, the works of Marín and the cantada composers go farther afield. The vocal range in most of these songs tends to be about a tenth, though it can be wider (e.g., a thirteenth in no. 20). Some songs are especially difficult to sing because of their unusual or chromatic skips and tricky rhythms. In general, all thirty-one songs in this collection are more demanding than French, Dutch, German, and English art songs of the time; but they are less demanding than the ornate Italian operatic songs. To what extent the written musical line was decorated with improvised ornaments is unknown at this time, but we can assume that this practice, so common in France and Italy, was also adopted by at least some Spanish singers.

The accompaniment required in these songs is always chordal (i.e., basso continuo, plus additional obbligato instruments in some cases). Although the songs (nos. 1–3) from the Ballard volumes call for lute accompaniment, the technique implied in no. 3 is more that of the strummed guitar than of the classically polyphonic French lute. The only works specifically calling for guitar accompaniment are nos. 4, 5, 12, and 13. In most of the remaining pieces the basso continuo instrument is not specified; but it is likely to have been the harp and/or organ, since harp and organ are specified as continuo instruments in nos. 17 and 26 and in many other polyphonic tonos and villancicos by the same composers. A "violón" (= cello) is sometimes named as an additional instrument, and in nos. 8 and 17 an independent violón line is given. An obbligato flute is part of the accompaniment in number 23; two violins are part of one of Durón's cantadas, no. 26, and an oboe and violin are required in two other cantadas (nos. 30 and 31).

The Composers

Juan Aranies (no. 4)

Born in Catalonia, Aranies studied in Alcalá de Henares, where he became a priest, and then in Rome. He was mestre de canto at Seo de Urgel Cathedral from 1627 until 1634 and perhaps again in 1649. In 1624, when the second volume of his Tonos y villancicos was published (the first volume is lost), he was a singer and chapel master to the Spanish community in Rome. His collection of vocal pieces with both basso continuo and independent guitar accompaniment is important because it is an example of Spanish influence in Italy at a time when Italian music had come to dominate Europe.[8]

José Asturiano (no. 7)

Little is known about this composer, who was a singer in the capilla real in Madrid in 1672. A few of his compositions survive in archives in Barcelona, Cuenca, and Guatemala.[9]

Henri de Bailly (no. 3)

A singer and lutenist, de Bailly was active at the court of France from 1609, when he became valet to King Henry IV, until his death in 1637. He served as head of the king's music chamber (*surintendant de la musique de la chambre du roi*) from at least 1625. He wrote music for several ballets printed in Gabriel Bataille's *Airs de differents autheurs, mis en tablature de luth*, vols. 5 and 6 (Paris, 1614–15), which is the source of no. 3 in this anthology. His choice of a Spanish text and guitar-like accompaniment may be the result of the vogue of Spanish culture at court. A man of considerable power, de Bailly was treated harshly by the French singer Bénigne de Bacilly,[10] who stated that he was a specialist "who dedicated himself entirely to the ornamentation of other men's works, without spending any time whatsoever at original composition."[11]

Gabriel Bataille (no. 2)

Although he may have been only an amateur through much of his life, Bataille was one of the most important musicians in Paris during the first third of the seventeenth century. He was the compiler and arranger of the solo airs that Pierre Ballard published as *Airs de cour mis en tablature de luth*, vols. 1–4 (1608–15), and thus he helped popularize these songs, which were sung and imitated throughout Europe. Bataille composed some of the songs himself, including airs for *ballets de cour*. His only known professional appointment was as one of two leaders of the queen's musical establishment; he held this post from 1619 until his death, in 1630. Bataille also composed four-voice airs and sacred songs, and he wrote poetry.[12]

Luis de Briceño (no. 5)

Nothing is known about Briceño except what appears in his important publication, the *Metodo mui facilissimo para apprender a tañer la guitarra*. He apparently was a Spaniard who was living in Paris at least during the year that the *Metodo* was published, 1626. Briceño's guitar book was important in popularizing the Spanish guitar and Spanish song in France. His collection was dedicated to Madame de Chales (variously spelled Chalais or Chalez), who may have been related to Henri de Talleyrand-Perigord, a close friend of Louis XIII. The *Metodo* is as important for its dance music as it is for its vocal music.[13]

Diego de and José de Cásseda (no. 8)

Diego de Cásseda flourished during the second half of the seventeenth century. He was *maestro de capilla* of the Pilar Cathedral in Saragossa and was succeeded upon his death, in September 1694, by Jerónimo Latorre. Since most compositions that are attributed to him have only the name Cásseda on the surviving manuscript, it is possible that they are, instead, by his son, José de Cásseda. José studied at the Pilar Cathedral in 1680 and afterwards served as *maestro de capilla* in the cathedral of Calahorra, in Pamplona (1691), and in Siguenza. From 1695 until at least 1698, he was back at the cathedral in Saragossa as chapel master. Later he was in Seville.[14]

Sebastián Durón (nos. 23–26)

Durón was born near Toledo in April 1660 and held posts early in his career in Seville (1680), Burgo de Osma (1685), and Palencia (1686). He joined the royal chapel in Madrid as an organist in 1691 and remained an important member of that chapel until 1706, when he was forced into exile in southern France for opposition to the new king, Philip V. He spent the rest of his life in Bayonne and its environs and died in Cambó on 3 August 1716. He was a prolific composer of both sacred and secular music. His *zarzuelas* show strong Italian influences, and he was among the first to introduce the cantata into Spain, for which he was duly chastised by more conservative Spanish music theorists.[15]

Juan Hidalgo (nos. 14–16)

The best-known composer of vocal music in Madrid in the second half of the seventeenth century, Hidalgo was born in the capital sometime between the years 1612 and 1616, and he died there on 30 March 1685. Hidalgo was active at the court as harpist and harpsichordist from 1631 until his death. Although he wrote much sacred vocal music, his secular songs, most of which were intended for the theater, are his most important works. Hidalgo's association with Pedro Calderón led to the first Spanish opera, *La púrpura de la rosa* (the music for which is lost) and in 1660 to the opera *Celos aun del aire matan* (the oldest Spanish opera whose music survives). Although he adopted the Italian recitative in his operas, his *tonos humanos* remain more faithful to traditional Spanish song than do those of Durón and Serqueira. Hidalgo also composed music for the earliest *zarzuela* whose music survives intact: *Los celos hacen estrellas* (1672), with words by Juan Vélez de Guevara.[16]

José Marín (nos. 11–13)

José Marín was born ca. 1619 and he died in 1699. The first record we have of his activities dates from 1644, when he entered the Encarnación Monastery in Madrid as a tenor. Although he was a priest, he must have led a colorful life. In 1654 and 1656 he was arrested for alleged robbery and murder and was whipped, unfrocked, and banished from Madrid for ten years. Despite all this, he seems to have led a productive life, and his obituary gives highest praise to his ability as a composer and performer. He wrote about sixty secular songs for solo voice and two secular duets, all of which are accompanied by guitar or another basso continuo instrument. No other seventeenth-century Spanish composer is known to have written so many solo *tonos humanos*.[17]

Juan de Navas (nos. 20–21)

There were several musicians with the name of Navas in Madrid in the second half of the seventeenth century, but the most important (and therefore the most likely to be the composer of the two songs in this anthology) was Juan de Navas, who was *maestro de la capilla real* in 1683 and who collaborated with Durón in the *zarzuela Apolo y Dafne*. There are other compositions for solo voice and accompaniment by de Navas in Madrid's Biblioteca Nacional. His father, Juan Francisco Gómez de Navas, was a royal harpist in 1669, and Juan, the son, was probably a harpist also. He wrote a letter of approbation in Fernando de Huete's harp manual of 1702. Although we do not know exactly when he died, extant records indicate that he was still alive in 1709.[18]

Juan de Paredes (no. 19)

Paredes was a *maestro de capilla* of the Descalzes Convent in Madrid during the second half of the seventeenth century. Although little is known about his life, we do know that he was already retired on 18 April 1705, when he contributed an approbation to a treatise on plain chant. He is not to be confused with Juan Bonet de Paredes (d. 1710), his exact contemporary. Only sacred works of his are known to have survived.[19]

Juan de Lima Serqueira (nos. 27–31)

Serqueira first appears as a harpist for a theater company in Granada in 1676, and we know he was active from later that year until at least 1719 in Madrid, where he performed in and composed for various theaters. He died after 1726.[20]

Juan del Vado (no. 17)

Juan del Vado flourished in Madrid between ca. 1625 and 1691. He was both organist and violinist in the *capilla real*, and he came from a family of violinists (his father, Felipe del Vado, joined the *capilla real* as a violinist in 1633, and his brother Bernardo joined the *capilla real* as a violinist in 1648). Although Juan del Vado was famous as a composer of secular *tonadas* during his own lifetime, he is known today for a large amount of sacred music, extant principally in two large manuscripts in the Madrid Biblioteca Nacional (Mus. MSS M. 1323–24), and for twenty-one masses in the archive of the cathedral of Avila.[21]

Matías Veana (no. 6)

A member of the Encarnación Monastery in Madrid in the mid-seventeenth century, Veana was *maestro* of the parish of Los Santos Juanes in 1677, when he successfully sought the top musical position at the Royal College of Corpus Christi in Valencia. Matías Veana's popularity spread to the Americas, and his works can be found there today, as well as in Barcelona and Montserrat.[22]

The Edition

For most of the songs in this volume, editorial emendation has been minimal, since the sources are almost completely free of error. The few necessary corrections in the music are indicated by means of brackets [ ] and/or are explained in the Critical Commentary. Parentheses surround editorial cautionary accidentals, and accidentals for the same pitch are not repeated within a measure in this edition, even though the accidental sign is repeated in the source.

When the accompanying instruments are clearly specified in the sources (e.g., harp, guitar, lute, etc.) the appropriate instrument is so indicated in the edition. In nos. 4 and 5, the direction of the note stem on a guitar chord indicates the direction of the strum. The organ was also a typical accompanying instrument for these pieces. One instrument would realize chords while another (e.g., the *violón*) played the bass line. The basso continuo realizations provided here in cue-size notation are all editorial suggestions. The editorial realizations aim for simplicity: basically contrapuntal entries are used only where clearly called for, and the style of the realizations has been kept consistent with that found in contemporary polyphonic songs. This style is characterized by a basically note-against-note texture, the use of two- or three-note chords, and a conservative harmonic vocabulary. The songs whose accompaniments appear as tablature in the source are here given as two-stave transcriptions. These songs are those taken from the guitar and lute books of Briceño, Ballard, and Marín, as well as the guitar version of Aranies's song (no. 4).

Songs 5, 30, and 31 have been largely reconstructed from fragments (see the Critical Commentary). In no. 5 the music for the voice has been reconstructed from a melodic row suitable for the *folía* harmony. In nos. 30 and 31 the basso continuo and obbligato violin and oboe parts have been reconstructed to suit the surviving vocal part and correspond to similar pieces by contemporary Spanish composers.

There are no dynamic signs in the sources and none have been added here. The few tempos contained in the sources are reproduced in this edition, but no new tempo indications have been added. Editorial suggestions for alternate rhythms for the voice in verses other than the first are given in cue-size notation. Thus, the singer must regard the determination of the proper tempo to be part of his/her interpretation.

Original phrase markings have been retained from the sources only when such markings are relevant in terms of modern performance. Editorial changes in phrasing are reported in the Critical Commentary.

Songs with the ₵ metrical sign in the prints or manuscripts are transcribed here with the same rhythmic values as in the sources. For songs whose sources have the 3 or ₵3 signature, however, the present transcription has reduced the note values to one fourth their original values. This transcription usually results in a quarter-note beat in $\frac{4}{4}$ and an eighth-note beat in $\frac{6}{8}$. The original barlines have been retained wherever they are given in the sources in accordance with modern practice. Otherwise, barlines have been added to fit the metrical accent or rhythmic pattern. Such additions are cited in the Critical Commentary.

Most texts in the present edition have been prepared from hand-written copies, made by the editor, of the original manuscripts. A few were prepared from microfilm or photocopies, whenever these could be obtained.

In the original manuscripts, the song texts are written out to the music in separate sections, often on different pieces of paper, and so poetic structure is not shown. At times, the additional *coplas* are written as if in prose rather than as poetry. Although very few present problems in discovering their stanzaic form, the order and repetition of the parts is frequently ambiguous. It is often unclear whether the *estribillo* is to precede the *coplas*, is to be repeated after each *copla* (or simply at intervals), or is to come only at the end of all the *coplas*. All these variations occur in printed poetic texts; but since the song texts are not copied as poems, the overall poetic structure must be determined from the sense of the text or by guesswork. The resolution of the problem in this edition depends first on any indication in the text, and second on the meaning of the song. Editorial suggestions are enclosed in brackets.

The translations aim to provide, whenever possible, a literal line-for-line, word-for-word rendition of the Spanish so that a singer who does not read Spanish may understand the meaning of the text. For this reason, every effort has been made to have each English line correspond to its Spanish counterpart. This has been impossible at times because of the Spanish construction that places the subject after the verb, a device which can be employed only rarely in English. In several cases in which the original is quite convoluted, it seemed best to paraphrase the sense rather than provide a literal translation.

Punctuation and capitalization have been modernized. This is true for spelling as well, except when a difference of pronunciation would have been involved (e.g., *mesmo* instead of *mismo*, which in no. 27 is needed for the rhyme). Except for bracketed portions, composer-names are given in the edition just as they appear in the source for each song.

Sources

The first five songs of this edition are taken from prints issued in the early seventeenth century; the remaining twenty-six songs are from manuscripts dating from between the mid-seventeenth century and the early eighteenth century. It would seem that none of these songs has been printed or reprinted since the beginning of the eighteenth century, with the exception of Marín's Pasacalle (no. 12), published in Pedrell's *Teatro lírico español*, vol. 3, and Serqueira's "Todo es amor" (no. 29), published (albeit, with only one *copla*) in Pedrell's *Teatro lírico español*, vols. 4–5.

The printed sources each have their own peculiarities, and these are described in the Critical Commentary. Briefly, Briceño's *Metodo* (1626) is primarily a guitar manual, containing guitar chords and text, but without vocal line. In Ballard's volumes of *airs de cour* (1609, 1614), for voice and lute accompaniment, the Spanish songs constitute only a fraction of the total contents. Aranies's *Libro segundo de tonos y villancicos* (1624) is scored for from one to four voices and indicates both continuo accompaniment and guitar chords. (Since these often conflict, they are obviously alternative rather than simultaneous versions of accompaniment.) The copies of the Briceño and Ballard books used for this edition are preserved in the Bibliothèque Nationale in Paris; the Aranies print is in the Civico Museo, Bologna.

Most of the source manuscripts are in partbook format, with each piece on loose pages folded together. In most of these sources a large sheet of paper is folded in half, with the *estribillo* on folio a and the *coplas* on folio d; the fold is at the top of folio a. The accompaniment is on folio a of another folded sheet of paper; the vocal folio is placed inside the accompaniment folio and then folded once more so that the octavo front folio can carry whatever title the copyist chose to place on it. Such folded bundles are commonplace in seventeenth-century Spanish musical archives. The manuscript sources for songs in the present edition come from archives in Cambridge, Venice, Madrid, Barcelona, Segovia, Cuenca, Valladolid, Palencia, Valencia, and Guatemala City. There is no reason to believe that any of these manuscript sources are autograph; instead they seem to be copies made by or for provincial *maestros*, and the dates that sometimes appear on these manuscripts presumably refer to date of copy or performance, rather than to date of composition.

Three manuscript sources differ from those manuscripts described above in that they each contain collections of songs, rather than being devoted to a single piece. The Trend Manuscript (Cambridge, Fitzwilliam Museum, MS MU4–1958) is an elaborate manuscript containing fifty songs in score with guitar accompaniments—all composed by José Marín. The Venice Manuscript (Biblioteca Nazionale Marciana, Music MS H.IV, 470 [=9994] [Cantarini]) is a large collection of anonymous pieces in score, though most of the solo songs can be identified through concordances as works by Juan Hidalgo or José Marín. Madrid Biblioteca Nacional, Music MS M. 2618 is a collection of works for voice, violin, oboe, and continuo, of which only the vocal partbook survives. All three of these sources are comprised primarily of solo works; however, they also contain some songs for two voices with accompaniment.

All sources are cited for each song in the Critical Commentary. Most pieces in the edition are taken from unique sources, but a few (nos. 12, 13, and 19) survive in more than one source. Number 12 exists in both the Trend Manuscript and in Madrid, Biblioteca Nacional, Music MS 3881. Despite the near identity of the two sources, the former has been used for the edition because it has a fully written-out accompaniment (guitar tablature) rather than a basso continuo line. Number 13 appears in both the Trend Manuscript and the Madrid, Biblioteca Nacional source. The Trend Manuscript has been used here, since the song exists only as a duet in the Madrid source. Number 19 survives in two sources (Segovia, Cathedral Archive, and Cuenca, Cathedral Archive) of equal primacy, and the choice of the Segovia manuscript as the source for this edition has been an arbitrary one.

John H. Baron
Daniel L. Heiple

Acknowledgments

This work was made possible by a summer research grant from the National Endowment for the Humanities and by a research grant from the American Council of Learned Societies. Particular thanks are due to Donna Dalferes MacGregor and Susan Lemmon for assistance in copying out the music, to Jack Sage, who located the most important José Marín manuscript for me, to the librarians, archivists, and *maestros de capilla* who opened up their archives to me, and to my wife, Doris, for many sacrifices so that I could complete this work.

John H. Baron

Notes

1. Felipe Pedrell, *Teatro lírico español*, vols. 3–5 (La Coruña, 1897–98).

2. José Marín, *Dos pasacalles para canto y guitarra*, ed. Graciano Tarragó (Madrid: Unión Musical Española, 1965); and Lope Felix de Vega Carpio, *Cinco canciones del siglo XVII*, ed. Graciano Tarragó (Madrid: Unión Musical Española, 1963).

3. Although Cristobal Galán wrote some magnificent solo art songs, none are included in this edition because they will be published in the forthcoming volume 4 of the eleven-volume *Collected Works of Cristobal Galán*, ed. John H. Baron and Daniel L. Heiple (Brooklyn: Institute of Medieval Music). Galán's "Ya los caballos de jazmín" is included in Miquel Querol's *Tonos humanos del siglo XVII* (Madrid: Editorial Alpuerto, 1977), pp. 23–24.

4. Durón was most severly criticized by Benito Jerónimo Feijóo, *Theatro critico universal*, (Madrid, 1726), 1:287. See A. Martín Moreno, "El P. Feijóo (1676–1764) y los músicos españoles del siglo XVIII," *Anuario Musical* 28–29 (1976): 221–42.

5. The word *villancico* had distinct meanings in different epochs. In its earliest usage it refers to the refrain of a song or poem, a short two-to-four-line poem that at one time existed as a separate song. In the sixteenth century, it refers to the whole song with the refrain and the *coplas* (that is, stanzas or verses), usually followed by a repetition of the refrain *(estribillo)*. Because of the Post-Tridentine practice of transforming popular secular material into religious and devotional literature, the *villancico* in the seventeenth century came to refer to a composition written for and performed in church on certain feast days. These compositions followed the same structure of refrain and verse as did the secular song. The refrain was no longer a popular ditty which was glossed by the composer and poet, but was composed along with the rest of the poem. Nowadays, the word *villancico* is used mainly in the expression *villancico de Navidad*, which is a carol sung at Christmas.

6. There is a rather extensive literature in Spanish on this type of poetry. J. G. Cummins's introduction to his anthology (*The Spanish Traditional Lyric* [Oxford: Pergamon Press, 1977]) will be most helpful to the English reader. It also has a bibliography for further reading.

7. The finest appreciative description of this poetry in either Spanish or English is Edward M. Wilson's "Spanish and English Religious Poetry of the Seventeenth Century," *Journal of Ecclesiastical History* 9 (1958): 38–53.

8. *The New Grove Dictionary of Music and Musicians*, s.v. "Arañés," by Robert Stevenson. See also Miguel Querol, *Cantatas y canciones para voz solista è instrumentos (1640–1760)*, vol. 5, pt. 1 of *Musica barroca española* (Barcelona: Consejo Superior de Investiga-ciones Cientificas, 1973), p. 33, parte musical, pp. 127–32; J. Pena and H. Anglés, *Diccionario de la música labor* (Barcelona: Editorial Labor, 1954); J. H. Baron, "Secular Spanish Solo Song in Non-Spanish Sources, 1599–1640," *Journal of the American Musicological Society* 30 (1977): 41.

9. Robert Stevenson, *Renaissance and Baroque Musical Sources in the Americas* (Washington, D.C.: OAS, 1970), p. 76; N. Alvarez Solar-Quintes, "Panorama musical desde Felipe III a Carlos II," *Anuario musical* 12 (1957): 197.

10. Bénigne de Bacilly, *Remarques curieuses* (Paris, 1668), trans. and ed. Austin B. Caswell, in Musical Theorists in Translation (Brooklyn: Institute of Medieval Music, 1968), 7:29.

11. M. Jurgens, *Documents de Minutier Central concernant l'histoire de la musique (1600–1650)* (Paris, n.d.), pp. 54–61; J. Anthony, *French Baroque Music* (New York, 1974), p. 339.

12. *The New Grove Dictionary of Music and Musicians*, s.v. "Gabriel Bataille," by J. Baron.

13. *Die Musik in Geschichte und Gegenwart*, s.v. "Briceño," by M. Querol; Baron, "Secular Spanish Solo Song," pp. 31–33.

14. Robert Stevenson, *Christmas Music from Baroque Mexico* (Berkeley, 1974), pp. 11 and 27; Pena and Anglés, *Diccionario*, p. 472; J. Lopez-Calo, "Corresponsales de Miquel de Irízar," *Anuario musical* 20 (1965): 231; J. G. Marcellán, *Palacio de Oriente, catálogo del Archivo de Música* (Madrid, n.d.), p. 166; Pedro Calahorra Martinez, *La música en Zaragoza en los siglos XVI y XVII* (Zaragoza: Institución "Fernando el Catolico," 1977–78), 1:72, 2:120–21.

15. *The New Grove Dictionary of Music and Musicians*, s.v. "Sebastián Durón," by J. Sage and J. Baron. For an example of Durón's zarzuelas, see S. Durón and José de Cañizares, *Salir el amor del mundo, zarzuela en dos journadas*, ed. A. Martín Moreno (Málaga, 1979), pp. 13–44.

16. *The New Grove Dictionary of Music and Musicians*, s.v., "Hidalgo," by J. Sage and J. Baron.

17. *The New Grove Dictionary of Music and Musicians*, s.v. "José Marín," by J. Baron.

18. Querol, *Cantatas y canciones*, pp. 11 and 12.

19. Pena and Anglés, *Diccionario*, p. 1716; J. I. Perdomo-Escobar, *El archivo musical de la Catedral de Bogotá* (Bogotá, 1976), p. 742.

20. *The New Grove Dictionary of Music and Musicians*, s.v., "Sequeiros," by Robert Stevenson.

21. Luis Robledo, "Los canones enigmaticos de Juan del Vado," *Revista de musicología* 3 (1982): 129–96.

22. R. Stevenson, *Musical Sources*, p. 103; Pena and Anglés, *Diccionario*, pp. 2205–6; Solar-Quintes, "Panorama," p. 190.

Critical Commentary, Texts, and Translations

The following section includes commentary on both the music and the texts of these songs. Abbreviations used below are as follows: M = measure; r.h. = right hand; l.h. = left hand. Pitch designations are given according to the Helmholtz system, wherein c′ = middle C; c″ = the C above middle C, and so forth.

[1] Air   (Anonymous)

1.   Decid cómo puede ser,
ojos, que estando mirando,
alegres estéis penando
y tristes mostréis placer.

    Tell me how it can be,
eyes, that when looking
happy you are suffering
and when sad you show pleasure.

2.   Decid, ojos, con engaño
vivís con mucho contento,
cómo tenéis sufrimiento
para pasar tantos daños.

    Tell me, eyes, through deceit
you live with great joy,
how you can have patience
to pass so many dangers.

3.   Y así pensáis merecer
el bien que estéis deseando:
alegres estéis penando
y tristes mostréis placer.

    And in this way you hope to deserve
the good you desire,
for when happy you are suffering,
and when sad you show pleasure.

4.   O qué bien sabéis fingir,
mostrando tener sosiego,
si en viendo dais a sentir
que abrasáis en vivo fuego.

    Oh, how well you know how to deceive
by showing a great calm,
if, when seeing, you give the feeling
that you burn with live fire.

5.   Sujetaos a padecer
lo que prendistes mirando:
alegres estéis penando
y tristes mostréis placer.

    Learn to suffer
what you ignited when looking:
for when happy, you are suffering
and when sad, you show pleasure.

SOURCE: Pierre Ballard, ed., *Airs de cour mis en tablature de luth*, vol. II (Paris, 1609): fols. 66ᵛ–67. See Baron, "Secular Spanish Solo Song," p. 31, where the similarity of this song to a song in three Modenese sources is pointed out.
  MUSIC: All barlines are editorial except for the double bars and those at the beginnings of the first endings.

[2] Air   (Gabriel Bataille)

1.   Si sufro por ti, morena,
mucho me place mi pena,
pues van tus ojos mirando,
al mismo sol admirando.

    If I suffer for you, dark lady,
my suffering pleases me a lot;
when your eyes are looking,
the sun itself is dazzled.

2.   ¿Qué te sirve, cruel Amor,
tormentarme[1] con dolor?,
pues que me place la pena
que sufro por mi morena.

    What does it profit you, cruel Love,
to torment me with pain,
since I enjoy the suffering
that I suffer for my dark lady?

3.   El mal que me haces sentir,
contento me hace vivir,

    The malady you make me feel
makes my life happy,

pues yo me huelgo en la pena	since I am content in the suffering
que sufro por mi morena.	that I suffer for my dark lady.

4.	Si jamás la olvidaré	If I never will forget her
	el tiempo que pasaré,[2]	all the time I shall live,
	contino haga la pena	make the suffering continuous
	pues déjame mi morena.[3]	and leave me my dark lady.

Source: Pierre Ballard, ed., *Airs de cour mis en tablature de luth*, vol. V (Paris, 1614): fols. 56ᵛ–57. The title of the particular *ballet de cour* from which this song comes is unknown, and it is found in Ballard's edition amidst various French excerpts from ballets most of which are untitled. Cf. Margaret McGowan, *L'Art du ballet de cour en France 1581–1643* (Paris: Editions CNRS, 1963), pp. 276–77.

Text: 1. Source has "Atromentarme," which is emended here for sense and scansion. 2. Source has "que yo pasaré," which is emended here for scansion. 3. Source has "pues dexe a mi morena," which is emended here for sense and scansion.

[3] Pasacalle: La folie   ([Henri] de Bailly)

1.	Yo soy[1] la locura,	I am Folly,
	la que sola infundo	who alone infuses
	placer y dulzura	pleasure, sweetness,
	y contento al mundo.	and joy in the world.
2.	Sirven a mi nombre	All serve in my name,
	todos mucho o poco,	great or small,
	y no, no hay hombre[2]	but not one of them
	que piense ser loco.	thinks he is mad.

Source: Pierre Ballard, ed., *Airs de cour mis en tablature de luth*, vol. V (Paris, 1614): fols. 57ᵛ–58. The title of the particular *ballet de cour* from which this song comes is unknown. See similar commentary for no. 2.

Music: M. 14, all parts, final note is dotted quarter.

Text: 1. Source has "o soy." 2. Source has "y pero no hay hombre," which has been emended for purposes of underlay.

[4] [Tono humano]   (Juan Aranies)

Estribillo

Dígame un requiebro,	Tell me a sweet nothing,
galán amador;	gallant lover;
dígame un requiebro;	tell me a sweet nothing;
dígame un amor.	tell me your love.

Coplas

1.	De cabellos de oro	With golden hair
	tejido[1] en cordón,	woven in a braid,
	estaba una niña	there was a girl
	que me cautivó.	who captivated me.
2.	Viéndome la niña	The girl, seeing me
	con tal turbación,	with such confusion,
	me dijo soltando	spoke to me, freeing
	la trenza[2] y la voz.	her braid and voice.
3.	Pero con los[3] ojos	But with my eyes
	hacia su blanco,	on their target,
	atiné cual ciego	I hit the mark like a blind man
	por el resplandor.[4]	guided only by the brightness.
4.	Lleguéme por ver	I drew near in order to see,
	más de cerca[5] el sol,	much closer the sun,
	y caí abrasado,[6]	and I fell burned,
	cual otro Faetón.[7]	like another Phaeton.

5. Su voz y palabra	With her voice and speech,
tal vista me dio	such a sight made for me
milagro pues hizo[8]	a miracle, since she created
por su boca amor.	love from her mouth.
6. Viéndome mortal	Seeing myself mortal
y ancho el corazón,	and my heart full,
di un suspiro al aire	I gave a sigh to the air
que al cielo llegó.	that reached heaven.
7. Con otro la niña	With another, the girl
al mío llegó,	reached mine,
diciendo corrida	asking, somewhat embarrassed,
si tan linda soy.	if she was that pretty.

SOURCE: Juan Aranies, *Libro segundo de tonos y villancicos* (Rome, 1624), no. 2.

MUSIC: Source indicates accompaniment either by guitar or by continuo, but not by the two simultaneously. Mm. 2 and 5, no guitar chords indicated here; editorial chords added to follow harmonies suggested by basso continuo, since continuation of previous chords would lead to severe clashes with the vocal part. Mm. 13 and 17, guitar, for rhythmic purposes the held chord has been restruck, although this is not indicated in the source.

TEXT: 1. Source has "texicado." 2. Source has "la trerzai." 3. Source has "las." 4. Source has "respandor." 5. Source has "cercar." 6. Source has "abrasad." 7. Source has "faton." 8. Source has "pue hzo."

[5] Folías   (Luis de Briceño)

Coplas

1. Volaba la palomita	The little dove flew
por encima del verde limón,	above the green lemon tree;
con las alas aparta las ramas,	with its wings it parts the branches,
con el pico lleva la flor.	with its bill it carries away the flower.
2. Arrojóme las manzanetas	[She] threw me the apples
por encima del manzanar;	over the apple tree;
arrojómelas y arrojéselas	[she] threw them to me and I threw them to her,
y tornómelas a arrojar.[1]	and [she] threw them back to me.
3. Si jamás duermen mis ojos,	If my eyes never find sleep,
madre mía, ¿qué harán?,	my mother, what will they do?
que como amor los desvela,	For as love keeps them awake,
pienso que se morirán.	I think they will die.
4. Quien dijo muerte al amor	He who said death to love
libre de pesares era;	was free from sorrow;
mejor dijera dolor	it would have been better to say pain,
y más natural le fuera.	and that would have been more natural for him.
5. Una mora en mí enamora,	A Moorish girl sets my heart on fire,
por ser mora de nación,	because she is a girl of the Moorish sect;
mas no es mora pues que mora	but she is not Moorish since
dentro de mi corazón.[2]	she dwells in my heart.

SOURCE: Luis de Briceño, *Metodo mui facilissimo para aprender a tañer la guitarra* (Paris, 1626).

MUSIC: Only the text of the vocal part exists in the source; music editorially reconstructed according to principles established in Baron, "Secular Solo Song," p. 27 (see The Edition above). The guitar chords are indicated in the source by letters, which are explained at the beginning of the *Metodo*.

TEXT: 1. J. G. Cummins, *The Spanish Traditional Lyric* (New York, 1977), pp. 3–7, discusses the meaning and delicacy of this stanza and its numerous variants in Golden Age literature. 2. This stanza involves a word-play on *mora*, which is both a noun, meaning "Moorish girl," and a verb, meaning "she dwells." The first line of the stanza plays with the same sounds in "enamora."

[6] Solo al Santísimo   (Matías Veana)

Estribillo

Ay, amor,
qué dulce tirano
te contemplo hoy,
   pues sujetas
a los más rebeldes
con dorados grillos
del más fino amor.
   Ay, amor,
que es gloria tu pena,
delicia el dolor.
   Ay, amor.

Oh, love,
what a sweet tyrant
I see in you today,
   for you subdue
the most rebellious
with golden shackles
of the finest love.
   Oh, love,
your suffering is glory,
your pain a delight.
   Oh, love.

Coplas

1.   Entre dulces
diliquios de un alma,
que afectos respira
de amante pasión,
   se perciben
los aires gustosos,
efectos gustosos[1]
que causa la unión.
   Ay, amor.

   Among the pleasant
swoonings of a soul
that breathes the emotions
of a lover's passion,
   are perceived
the pleasurable breezes,
the pleasurable effects
that cause the union.
   Oh, love.

2.   ¿Hasta cuándo,
o Esposo, decías
entre obscuros velos
he de ver tu amor?,
   y la tela
que oculta el enigma
no rasgas que sea
despojo del sol.[2]
   Ay, amor.

   But when,
my Husband, did you say
I will see your love
among the dark veils?
   And the cloth
that hides the enigma
you do not tear so it will not be
a spoil from the sun.
   Oh, love.

3.   O si rostro
a rostro te viese,
o penosa ausencia,
o fuerte dolor,
   pues violenta
mi alma se halla
entre las cadenas
de humana pasión.
   Ay, amor.

   If face
to face I could see you,
o painful absence,
o strong pain,
   since my soul
finds itself violent
among the chains
of human passion.
   Oh, love.

4.   Derribad,
mi amado, la cárcel
que así me detiene
cansada y sin voz,
   para ir
a ese alcázar celeste,
glorioso palacio,
divina región.
   Ay, amor.

   Raze,
my beloved, the jail
that thus holds me
tired and without voice,
   so I can go
to that celestial fortress,
the glorious palace,
the divine region.
   Oh, love.

5.   Si ablando
y atendo tus finezas,
flechadme suave
el más fuerte arpón,
   que la muerte
de tan dulce tiro

   If I soften
and wait on your favors,
shoot me gently
with the strongest spear,
   since death
from such a sweet shot

es vida perpetua	is perpetual life
de mi corazón.	for my heart.
Ay, amor.	Oh, love.

6.   Baste, baste,   Enough, enough,

señor de dulzuras,	lord of sweetness,
que es grande la herida	for the wound is great
y más el ardor,	and more so the fire,
y no hay fuerza	and there is no force
que resistir pueda	that can resist
a impulsos divinos	from divine impulses
tal llama mayor.	such a great flame.
Ay, amor.	Oh, love.

SOURCE: Valladolid, Cathedral Music Archive.
TEXT: 1. The copyist presumably repeated "gustosos." 2. There seems to be an error in the copy in these two lines; however, they have been allowed to stand here.

[7] Solo al Sacramento   (José Asturiano)

Estribillo

Céfiros blandos,	Gentle breezes,
líquidas fuentes,	liquid fountains,
ta, que descansa,	hush, for he rests,
ta, que se duerme	hush, for he falls asleep
a las fatigas	from the fatigue
de mis desdenes	of my disdain,
fiero Cupido—	this savage Cupid—
no le despierten.	do not awaken him.

Coplas

1.

Músicas celestes voces	Let the breezes sound and polish
céfiros pulan y suenen;	the celestial musical voices;
pájaros se oigan qué dulces	let the birds hear how sweet
cánticos místicos fuertes.	and loud the mystic songs.
Músicas voces,	Musical voices,
céfiros suenen,	breezes sound,
pájaros dulces,	sweet birds,
cánticos fuertes.	loud songs.

2.

Máximo empeño la cifra,	Let the cipher be a maximum pledge,
término la oculta breve,	the hidden long note an ending,
músico amor, blando cisne,	musical love, a gentle swan,
cándido extático fénix.	a white ecstatic phoenix.
Máxima cifra,	Maximum cipher,
término breve,	brief ending,
músico cisne,	musical swan,
cándido fénix.	white phoenix.

3.

Próvido amor como sabio	Provident love, as a wise man,
púrpura preciosa vierte,	pours forth precious scarlet,
tósigo que armoniza al malo,	venom that cures the sick,
báculo que alcanza al débil.	a staff that reaches the weak.
Próvido sabio	Provident wise man,
púrpura vierte,	pours forth scarlet,
tósigo al malo,	venom to the evil,
báculo al debil.	a staff to the weak.

4.

Sólida piedra la basa,	A solid stone is the base,
fábrica y muro tan fuerte,	construction and walls so strong,
única ofrece tu obra	your unique work offers
dórico al alma su albergue.	its doric refuge to the soul.
Sólida basa,	Solid base,
fábrica fuerte,	strong construction,

única obra,
dórico albergue.

5.   Ángeles puros y hombres
águilas a su luz vuelen;
Hércules amantes triunfen;
víboras en cantos huellen.
        Ángeles y hombres,
        águilas vuelen,
        Hércules triunfen,
        víboras huellen.

SOURCE: Cuenca, Cathedral Archive.

unique work,
doric refuge.

Let pure angels and men
fly as eagles in its light;
let Herculean lovers triumph;
let them in song tread asunder the perfidious.
        Let angels and men
        fly as eagles,
        triumph as Hercules,
        tread asunder the perfidious.

[8] Solo al Santísimo   ([Diego de or José de] Cásseda)

Estribillo

A las cortes de amor,
corazones, corazones,
venid, volad, corred;
la obediencia sin ojos
traiga, traiga la fe.

To the courts of love,
hearts, spirits,
come, fly, run;
let faith bring
blind obedience.

Coplas

1.   En el solio de un abril,
el rey de la majestad
del orbe los gran obrazos
ha mandado convocar.

In the throne of an April,
the king of majesty
has ordered to be convened
the great works of the world.

2.   Celebrar quiso las cortes
en esta estancia real,
que por honrar a María
siempre fue de celebrar.

He wanted to hold court
in this royal dwelling,
which, because it honors Mary,
was always to be celebrated.

3.   Su sangre y carne propone
para remedio eficaz
en las cortes que ocasiona
un contrafuero de Adán.

He proposes his blood and flesh
as an effective remedy
in the session caused
by Adam's breach of law.

4.   Es el día de las cortes
al Corpus y a quien leal
no asistiera, su justicia
declaró por consumar.

It is the day of court
on Corpus Christi, and on him who
does not faithfully attend,
he declared his justice to be done.

5.   Rinden humilde homenaje,
pero con ganancia tal,
que si un vasallo se ofrece,
es un reino lo que da.

They render humble homage,
but with such gain
that if a vassal offered himself,
it is a kingdom which he gives.

6.   El servicio que le hacen
es amor; la voluntad
fácilmente, pues, consiste
sólo en querer el amar.

The service they give him
is love; the will
easily consists then
only in wanting to love.

7.   Cada ley de su fineza
prodigio a pascuas será,
¿qué mucho si en esta octava/fiesta[1]
las maravillas están?

Each law of his finesse
will be a prodigy at Easter;
why wonder if on this feast day
the miracles occur?

8.   A dos fueros la observancia
se ha de reducir no más:
en el adorar servir
y en el temer confiar.

To two precepts the observance,
and no more, can be reduced:
in adoring, to serve,
and fearing, to trust.

9.   Grandes mercedes promete
rey que usó tanto veras,

The king that used so much truth
promises great gifts,

por su humildad asistir
y por su alteza el honrar.

through his humility to attend
and through his majesty to honor.

SOURCE: Valladolid, Cathedral Music Archive.
MUSIC: M. 4, continuo, note 3 omitted. M. 5, continuo, note 4 omitted. M. 17, voice, notes 4 and 5 each preceeded by sharp symbols. M. 39, voice and violin, note is a half-note.
TEXT: 1. The words "octava" and "fiesta" alternate in the source.

[9] Tono humano   (Anonymous)

Coplas

1.   Es el amor, ay, ay,
dulce prisión, ce, ce,
que al corazón, ta, ta,
le hace feliz, que, que,
pues en amante ley,
se mira el amor
en el mismo arder.

   Love is, oh, oh,
a sweet prison, hey, hey,
which makes, sh, sh,
the heart happy, uh, uh,
since in amorous law,
love is seen
in the very burning.

2.   No es su cadena, ay, ay,
pena fatal, ce, ce,
que es su rigor, ta, ta,
el halagar, que, que,
pues en su halago ves,
se mira el sufrir
por feliz placer.

   His chain is not, oh, oh,
a fatal sorrow, hey, hey,
for his severity, sh, sh,
is flattery, uh, uh,
since as you see in his flattery,
suffering is seen
by happy pleasure.

3.   En su prisión, ay, ay,
sabe el amor, ce, ce,
al padecer, ta, ta,
dar el sufrir, que, que,
pues en el padecer,
se mira el sentir
como dulce ley.

   In his prison, oh, oh,
love knows how, hey, hey,
to give suffering, sh, sh,
to suffering, uh, uh,
since in suffering,
feeling is seen
as a sweet law.

4.   Vino el amor, ay, ay,
en el arpón, ce, ce,
logra el rendir, ta, ta,
todo blasón, que, que,
pues en su esquivez,
se mira el rendir
sin querer querer.

   Love came, oh, oh,
in the spear, hey, hey,
every shield, sh, sh,
achieves rendition, uh, uh,
since in his coyness,
rendition is seen
without wanting to love.

SOURCE: Segovia, Cathedral Archive.
MUSIC: The source has barlines only in the vocal part. They occur at the end of each musical phrase (in mm. 2, 4, 6, 8, 10) and after each m. from m. 12 to the end.

[10] Solo a la vida humana   (Anonymous)

Estribillo

   Esta es la justicia
que manda hacer
amor poderoso,
de las almas rey,
a un hombre infelice
porque quiso bien.

   This is the punishment
that all-powerful love,
king of all souls,
orders for
an unhappy man
because he loved faithfully.

Coplas

1.   Manda que el rigor le saque
de la casa de su bien
con cadena sin las sogas
y con grillos en los pies.

   He orders that severity pull him
from his comfortable house
with chains, but without nooses,
and with shackles on his feet.

2. Manda que crüel ministro
    con rigurosa altivez
    sus temores acompañe
    al suplicio de una fe.

3. Manda que en tristes memorias
    de este adorado desdén,
    aunque ha siglos de pesares,
    un instante de placer.

4. Manda que en la revista
    no aguarde remedio aquél
    que por elogio y la envidia
    condenado embista fe.

5. Manda en fin a la desdicha
    de amor riguroso juez
    que le oblique a suspirar,
    a morir y a padecer.

SOURCE: Segovia, Cathedral Archive.

He orders that the cruel minister
with severe arrogance
accompany his fears
to the execution of his faith.

He orders in sad memories
of this beloved disdain,
even though he has centuries
of suffering, an instant of pleasure.

He orders that in the review
there be no help for him who
through praise and envy
is condemned for attacking faith.

The severe judge condemns him
at last to the wretchedness of love,
for he is ordered to sigh,
languish, and suffer.

[11] Tonada sola (José Marín)

Estribillo

Aguas de Manzanares,[1]
que alegres corréis,
¿quién pensara tan triste
que os volviera a ver?

Cuando me partí
de vuestros cristales,
de ausencia los males
amante sentí.

Aguas de Manzanares,
que alegres corréis,
¿quién pensara tan triste
que os volviera a ver?

Y hoy vuelvo sin mí
con nueva pasión,[2]
firme en la afición,
mudable en la fe.

Waters of the Manzanares,
who run happily,
who would think that I, so sad,
would return to see you?

When I went away
from your crystal waters,
as a lover I suffered
the evils of absence.

Waters of the Manzanares,
who run happily,
who would think that I, so sad,
would return to see you?

And today I return, beside myself
with a new passion,
firm in loving,
changeable in faith.

Coplas

1. De eligante Guadarrama
    pisaba la frente helado,[3]
    cuando a las puertas de abril
    esta valla mandó el año.

2. Deshecha en vidrios la nieve,
    gozaban ya los peñascos,
    de la prisión del invierno
    la libertad del verano.

3. Bajaban desde las cumbres
    los arroyos desatados
    a guarnecer con aljófar
    las nuevas galas del prado.

4. Triste balaba el pastor,
    cuando se alegraban tantos,
    porque no hacer lo que todos
    es pasión de un desdichado.

From the imposing Guadarrama
as ice it adorned the facade,
when at the gates of April
the year sent this obstacle.

With the snow melted in crystals,
the cliffs then enjoyed,
free from the prison of winter,
the liberty of summer.

The streams unleashed
flowed down from the peaks
to embellish with dew
the new trappings of the field.

Sadly the shepherd bleated
while the others rejoiced,
because not acting like the rest
is the suffering of an unfortunate.

5.   Y descubriendo entre flores
de Manzanares los campos,
a sus aguas sus tristezas
así les dijo cantando:

And disclosing among the flowers
the fields of the Manzanares,
he related his sorrows
to the waters, singing thus:

SOURCE: Segovia, Cathedral Archive.

MUSIC: M. 5, continuo, note 4 has sharp. M. 10, vocal part clearly indicates a $\frac{9}{8}$ measure by means of barlines (rare in the rest of the manuscript) and black notation; continuo has no barlines and black notes only for the two middle notes. M. 28, continuo, instead of the A here, there are two black quarter-notes (D, E).

TEXT: 1. Manzanares is a river that runs through Madrid; it was not necessary to use the definite article with the names of rivers in seventeenth-century Spanish. 2. This new passion ("nueva pasión") is sadness because his beloved, before cold as ice, has now warmed up to someone else, completely dashing his hopes. 3. The word "helado" is unclear in the source.

[12] Pasacalle del 5° tono de 3 para el tono   (José Marín)

Coplas

1.   Diz[1] que era como una nieve,
Marica,[2] la de Berlinches,
y viene el demonio y que hace
que su mal gusto la tizne,
    porque a todos dice
    que es para ella
    el peor ninguno,
    el mejor cualquiera.

They say she was like the snow,
that Marica from Berlinches,
and along comes the Devil
and has his bad taste smudge her,
    for she says to everyone
    that for herself she'll have
    none of the worst,
    anyone of the best.

2.   Era Marica en su aldea,
a la que inventó los esquinces,[3]
y quiso dar en ser onza
cansada[4] y ha de ser tigre,[5]
    porque a todos, etc.

She was Marica in her town,
the one where they invented slits,
and she wanted to be an [exact]
ounce [lynx], but she has to be a tiger,
    for she says, etc.

3.   Llegó Benito de fuera,
zagal de pocos abriles,
muy pobre para mudable
y muy verde para firme,
    porque a todos, etc.

Benito came from afar,
a shepherd of few years,
too poor to be fickle,
too green to be stern,
    for she says, etc.

4.   De este corazón se paga
porque tal vez lo que eligen
las presumidas de hermosas
algún diablo se lo dice,
    porque a todos, etc.

She is pleased with his love
because perhaps the choice
of would-be beauties
is dictated by a devil.
    for she says, etc.

5.   Con éste quiere casarse[6]
para que nadie la envidie,[7]
aprisionando lo hermoso[8]
con retención de lo libre,[9]
    porque a todos, etc.

She wants to marry him
so no one will envy her,
imprisoning her beauty,
but retaining her freedom,
    for she says, etc.

6.   Para la beca de esposo
le hace pruebas[10] de apacible,
pues antes para cordero[11]
que para pastor le elige,[12]
    porque a todos, etc.

For the position of husband
she gives him tests of tameness,
since she chooses him for a sheep,
rather than a shepherd,
    for she says, etc.

SOURCE: Cambridge, Fitzwilliam Museum, MS MU4–1958 (Trend MS), fols. 11–12^v.
CONCORDANCE: Madrid, Biblioteca Nacional, Music MS 3881, no. 34.
EDITION: Felipe Pedrell, *Teatro lírico español*, 3:47–48.

MUSIC: Strophes 2–6 are written after the *copla* score, not with the vocal part in Trend MS. Barlines occur in the source after every three eighth-note beats in Trend MS.

TEXT: 1. "Diz" is a colloquial form meaning *dicen* (= they say). 2. In modern Spanish "Marica" also refers to a male homosexual. 3. "Esquinces" is not found in any dictionary; *esquinzar* means "to shred." 4. "Onza cansada" makes little sense, but both sources have this reading; undoubtedly a play on *onza*, meaning both "ounce" and "lynx," is intended. 5. The poet uses "tigre" here because it gives the image of "spotted" or "stained." 6. This line is re-phrased "Casarse con el presente" in the Madrid MS. 7. The sense of this is that he is not that good a catch. 8. Madrid MS has the synonymous "lo bello" instead of "lo hermoso." 9. This line implies that she will play around in spite of being married. 10. This phrase is "pruevas le hace" in Madrid MS. 11. In Madrid MS this line is "con que a su favor por manso" (= so that with his favor as a sheep), playing on "manso" as "lead sheep" and "willing cuckold." 12. This line is "más que por pastor le admite" (= more than as a shepherd does she accept him) in the Madrid MS.

[13] Pasacalle del 3° tono de 3 para este tono (José Marín)

Estribillo

No sé yo cómo es,
que[1] quiero y no quiero
y quisiera querer.

I do not know how it is,
for I love and I don't love
and I would like to love.

Coplas

1. Yo siento un no sé que diga
    ansioso de helar[2] y arder
    que con él no acierto[3] a estar
    y no puedo estar sin él;
    no sé yo cómo es, etc.

    I feel an anxious I don't know
    what of freezing and burning,
    for I do not manage to have it
    and I cannot be without it.
    I do not know, etc.

2. Una atención descuidada,
    un temor que ignora ley,
    un sacrificio sin culto,
    y una adoración sin fe;
    no sé yo cómo es, etc.

    A careless attention,
    fear that ignores rules,
    a sacrifice without a service,
    adoration without faith.
    I do not know, etc.

3. Un escuchar, un oir,
    sin sobresalto el desdén,
    hacer[4] cuidado el descuido
    y dudar para creer;
    no sé yo cómo es, etc.

    To listen, to hear,
    disdain without shock,
    to be careful in being careless
    and to doubt in order to believe.
    I do not know, etc.

4. ¿Qué desaliñada flecha
    abrió[5] el corazón cruel,
    que me halaga siendo mal
    y atormenta siendo bien?,
    no sé yo cómo es, etc.

    What careless arrow
    opened my cruel heart,
    which pleases me when I am sick
    and torments me when I am well?
    I do not know, etc.

5. Miro sin odio mi culpa,
    y con odio alguna vez
    huyo el peligro y lo busco,
    y sólo llego a entender:[6]
    no sé yo cómo es, etc.

    I look with disgust upon my blame,
    and with disgust sometimes
    I flee danger and look for it,
    and I only come to understand:
    I do not know, etc.

SOURCE: Cambridge, Fitzwilliam Museum, MS MU 4–1958 (Trend MS), fols. 87ᵛ–90.
CONCORDANCE: Madrid, Biblioteca Nacional, Music MS 3881, no. 32, as a duet.
MUSIC: M. 15, continuo, r.h., this ornament apparently is an ascending slide (see Robert Donington, *The Interpretation of Early Music* [London: Faber & Faber, 1963], p. 572, and *The New Grove Dictionary of Music and Musicians*, s.v. "Ornaments"). M. 21, continuo, r.h., note 3, this ornament apparently is an ascending slide. Mm. 32–34 and 55–57, voice, rests omitted in source. Mm. 32–34, guitar, rhythm of these mm. is:

M. 42, strophes 2–5 written after the *copla* score.

Text: 1. Madrid MS has "pues" (= since) instead of "que." 2. Source has "declar," a nonsense word, instead of "de helar"; emended here after the Madrid MS. 3. Source has "haciera," a nonsense verb form, instead of "acierto"; emended here after Madrid MS. 4. Madrid MS has the unintelligible "ser más" (= to be more) instead of "hacer." 5. Madrid MS has "hirió" (= wounded) instead of "abrió." 6. Madrid MS has "temer" (= fear) instead of "entender."

[14] Solo a nuestra Señora (Juan Hidalgo)

Estribillo

Luceros y flores,	Stars and flowers,
arded y lucid,	burn and shine
al ver una aurora	when you see a dawn
que ilustra el zafir.	that brings glory to the sapphire.

Coplas

1.   Las flores del cielo ardan;   Let the flowers of heaven burn;
los astros del campo brillen;   let the stars of the field shine;
y exhalando sus alientos   and exhaling their breath
en esferas y pensiles,   in spheres and gardens,
    las flores ardan,   let the flowers burn,
    los astros brillen.   let the stars shine.

2.   Las rosas sus rayos copien;   Let the roses copy their rays;
los orbes sus luces pinten;   let the orbs paint their lights;
pues no imitan sus reflejos   since their reflections do not imitate
con el claro sus perfiles,   their profiles with clarity,
    las rosas copien,   let the roses copy,
    los orbes pinten.   let the orbs paint.

3.   La estrella a sus ojos muere;   The star dies before its eyes;
el alba al valiente vive;   the dawn lives for the valiant;
que a la luz de sus candores   for at the light of its whiteness
en encuentros tan felices,   in such happy encounters,
    la estrella muere,   the star dies,
    el alba vive.   the dawn lives.

4.   Luceros su planta huella;   Its step tramples the stars;
claveles su vista tiñe;   its vision colors the carnations;
pues con puras inflüencias   since with pure influences
en milagros de matices,   in miracles of tints,
    luceros huella,   it treads the stars,
    claveles tiñe.   it colors the carnations.

5.   Tinieblas intacta vence;   Intact it conquers the darkness;
reflejos constante ciñe;   constant it surrounds reflections;
que su frente con lo hermoso   for its forehead with beauty
en discordias apacibles,   in pleasant discord
    tinieblas vence,   conquers darkness,
    reflejos ciñe.   surrounds reflections.

6.   Los pechos amante hiere;   A lover, it strikes breasts;
las almas piadosa rije;   faithful, it governs souls;
pues con flechas poderosas   since with powerful arrows,
dando vida a quien la sirve,   giving life to him who serves it,
    los pechos hiere,   it strikes breasts,
    las almas rije.   it governs souls.

Source: Segovia, Cathedral Archive.
Music: M. 8–m.11, note 1, continuo, part is lacking in source; reconstructed here by analogy with previous mm. M. 10, voice, note 1 is an eighth-note.

[15] Al Santísimo Sacramento   (Juan Hidalgo)

Coplas

1.   Aves que al sol despertáis
de su cuna de clavel,
amad y sabed de mí
que quiero hasta no saber,
    que yo quiero bien
    a aquel que me quiere
    sin darle a entender
    que yo quiero bien.

      Birds that awaken the sun
from his cradle of carnations,
love and know from me
that I love more than I know,
    for I love well
    him who loves me,
    without letting him know
    that I love well.

2.   Quiero bien a una azucena;
entre cara candidez,
siento mis ojos helarse
y mi corazón arder,
    que yo quiero bien, etc.

      I love well a lily;
among precious whiteness
I feel my eyes freeze
and my heart burn,
    for I love well, etc.

3.   Quiero bien a aquel maná
que preservado se ve
de las injusticias del tiempo
con desagravio[1] del ser,
    que yo quiero bien, etc.

      I love well that manna,
for it is seen to be preserved
from the injustices of time
with reparation of being,
    for I love well, etc.

4.   Quiero bien a aquel zagal,
que no le permito ser
de los ojos míos cuando
galán de mis ojos es,
    que yo quiero bien, etc.

      I love well that boy,
for I do not let him be
my lover when
he is the apple of my eye,
    for I love well, etc.

SOURCE: Valladolid, Cathedral Archive.
MUSIC: M. 2, voice, note 2 is a quarter-note. M. 4, voice, note 1 has a sharp symbol.
TEXT: 1. Source has "un agravio" (= an offense) instead of "desagravio."

[16] Tono humano   (Juan Hidalgo)

Estribillo

   Viva mi esperanza
pues que llego a ver
la deidad de Filis,
que algún día fue
ingrata tirana,
más benigna, y pues
mi grande fortuna
pudo merecer
de Filis favores,
publique mi fe;
viva mi esperanza
pues ya llego a ver
que en Filis no hay
rigor ni desdén.

      May my hope live long,
since I come to see
the deity of Phyllis,
who one day was
an ungrateful tyrant,
more benign, and since
my great fortune
came to deserve
favors from Phyllis,
spread my faith;
long live my hope,
since I now come to see
that in Phyllis there is
neither rigor nor disdain.

Coplas

1.   Dulcísimo dueño mío,
perdona si te agravié
en blasonar que soy tuyo,
pues mi esperanza ha de ser
    servir para amar
    postrado a tus pies.

      My most sweet master,
pardon me if I offended you
in announcing that I am yours,
for my hope has to be
    to serve in order to love,
    prostrate at your feet.

2. Con tus luceros alumbras
toda un alma a que se ve
en las tinieblas de un ciego,
y pues me enseño a querer:
    viva mi esperanza
    por siglos, amén.
	With your stars you light
	all of a soul that sees itself
	in the darkness and blind,
	and since I teach myself to love:
	    long live my hope
	    for centuries, amen.

3. Sola tú, dueño querido,
me has cautivado; no des
al pensamiento malicias,
pues ves que no puede ser,
    pues sólo tú sola
    mi dueño has de ser.
	Only you, beloved master,
	have captivated me; do not give
	suspicions to my thought,
	since you see that it cannot be,
	    since only you alone
	    have to be my master.

SOURCE: Valencia, Cathedral Archive.
MUSIC: M. 25, voice, notes 4 and 5 are missing in the source. M. 27, all parts, final note is a half-note.

[17] Tonada a San Francisco   (Juan del Vado)

La más pura azucena su afecto ennobleció por preservarle siempre el intacto candor, porque no tienen impressiones de sombras tu cánido fulgor.	Your love ennobled the most pure lily by preserving in it forever its whole whiteness, because shadowy impressions do not have your white brilliancy.

SOURCE: Valladolid, Cathedral Music Archive.
MUSIC: Mm. 15–16, voice, the bracketed notes are missing in the source; added here by analogy with mm. 12–13. There are no additional *coplas*.

[18] Solo y acompañamiento   (Anonymous)

Con amantes inquietudes, Teresa, de suave incendio, surca, vence, logra, busca, mares, vicios, triunfos, puertos: surca mares, vence vicios, logra triunfos, busca puertos.	With a lover's anxieties, Theresa, of gentle fire, furrow, conquer, achieve, search for seas, vices, triumphs, harbors: furrow the seas, conquer vices, achieve triumphs, search for harbors.

SOURCE: Valladolid, Cathedral Music Archive.
MUSIC: M. 5, voice, slur between notes 2 and 3. M. 8, continuo, notes 1 and 2 are missing, making the m. short by one beat. M. 9, continuo, note 1 is a quarter-note. There are no additional *coplas*.

[19] Solo al Santísimo   ([Juan de] Paredes)

Estribillo

Si entre flores hermosas áspides andan y la vida cautivan con lo que halagan, ¡flores al arma!, ¡fuentes al arma!, ¡aves al arma! Ande alerta el cuidado por la campaña. Flores, fuentes, aves, ¡al arma, al arma!	If among the beautiful flowers asps crawl and they captivate life with their flattery, on guard, flowers! on guard, springs! on guard, birds! Have care, walk vigilant over the field of battle. Flowers, springs, birds, on guard, on guard!

Ande alerta el cuidado por la campaña.	Have care, walk vigilant over the field of battle.

Coplas

1. Formen[1] frente de banderas
    los jazmines en hileras
    al puro clavel[2] triunfante,
        sol radiante
    que en la nieve ostenta llamas.
        ¡Flores, al arma, al arma!

    Let the jasmine flowers in rows
form an advance line of streamers
for the pure, triumphant carnation,
    a radiant sun
that in the snow flashes flames.
    Flowers, on guard, on guard!

2. La preciosa artillería
    haga hermosa batería
    en perlas que se derraman
        y se inflaman
    en la hoguera que amor fragua.
        ¡Fuentes, al arma, al arma!

    Let the precious artillery
make a beautiful battery
of pearls that pour forth
    and take fire
in the blaze that love forges.
    Springs, on guard, on guard.

3. El pelicano[3] amoroso
    sea el sacre generoso
    que al ave nocturna y fiera[4]
        en su hoguera
    siempre tenga aprisionada.
        ¡Aves, al arma, al arma!

    Let the loving pelican
be the noble falcon,
which always holds imprisoned
    in his fire
the savage, nocturnal bird.
    Birds, on guard, on guard!

4. Este tulipán nevado
    de real púrpura listado
    descubra cual centinela
        la cautela
    que en el campo se derrama.
        ¡Flores, al arma, al arma!

    Let this snowy tulip
banded with royal crimson
discover as a sentinel
    the caution
that is poured forth in the field.
    Flowers, on guard, on guard!

5. Fosos sean de cristales
    cuantos vierta en manantiales
    la vista que al sol entrega
        lince y ciega
    de la fe dichosa esclava.
        ¡Fuentes, al arma, al arma!

    Let the trenches hold crystal waters,
however many the sight pours forth
in springs which it,
    both keen-sighted and blind,
as a blessed slave of faith, gives to the sun.
    Springs, on guard, on guard!

6. Nido pobre al fénix[5] de oro
    de mi pecho condecoro,
    formando ardor su[6] desvelo
        de mi hielo
    cuando le acuartela el alma.
        ¡Aves, al arma, al arma!

    I award from my breast
a poor nest for the golden phoenix,
creating ardor with care
    from my coldness
when my soul billets him.
    Birds, on guard, on guard!

SOURCE: Segovia, Cathedral Archive.
CONCORDANCE: Cuenca, Cathedral Archive.
MUSIC: The figures in the continuo are all from the Cuenca MS except for those in mm. 11 and 29; the source has a figure 6 in m. 24 under note 3, but this seems to be an error. M. 9, beat 4–m. 10, continuo is as follows in Cuenca:

M. 11, continuo, the bass figure appears only in the source. M. 23, voice, slur between notes 4 and 5.
TEXT: The poem presents all of nature as an army militantly proclaiming the faith. 1. Cuenca has "Ponen" (= place) instead of "Formen." 2. The carnation ("clavel") is a symbol of Christ's sacrifice. 3. The pelican ("pelicano") is a symbol of Christ's sacrifice. 4. The savage, nocturnal bird ("ave noctura y fiera") is a symbol of the devil. 5. The phoenix ("fénix") is a symbol of Christ's death and resurrection. 6. Cuenca has "amor con" (= love with) instead of "ardor su."

[20] Solo al Santísimo Sacramento   ([Juan de] Navas)

Estribillo

Ay, divino amor,
que fluctuando mares,
rémora de ti mismo,
seguro puerto hallaste.
A tu obediencia siempre
te rindan vasallaje
los prados y las selvas,
los montes y los valles.

Oh, divine love,
floating on the sea,
your own best obstacle,
you found a safe port.
Let the fields and forests,
the mountains and the valleys
always render service
to your obedience.

Coplas

1. Deidad por lo encendido
    de sus actividades,
    se abrasa mariposa
    quien salamandra[1] yace.

    A deity by the fieriness
    of his activities,
    he who reposes as a salamander
    is burned as a butterfly.

2. Aun más de lo imposible
    hoy en tu pecho hallaste,
    si de antiguas cenizas,
    nuevo fénix[2] renace.

    Even more of the impossible
    did you find today in your breast,
    if from ancient ashes,
    he is born as a new phoenix.

3. De un pecho enamorado
    vences dificultades;
    fue siempre atrevimiento
    hacer su amor cobarde.

    From an impassioned breast,
    you conquer difficulties;
    it was always daring to make
    one's love cowardly.

4. Al viento da las velas
    de tus felicidades,
    pues ya en su centro vive
    quien muere por amante.

    Put the sails of your
    happiness to the breeze,
    since he who dies as a lover
    now lives in his center.

5. Decirle que bien quiera
    muy bien puede escusarse,
    si amándose a sí mismo,
    correspondiente se hace.

    One can be excused
    from telling him to love well,
    if by loving himself,
    his love is reciprocated.

6. Navega viento en popa,
    pues eres hoy la nave
    fiel deseado puerto
    queriéndole lograste.

    Sail with an aft wind,
    since today you are the ship
    that by wanting it, found
    the trusting, desired harbor.

SOURCE: Valladolid, Cathedral Music Archive.
MUSIC: M. 1, continuo, note 3 has a sharp sign over it.
TEXT: 1. The salamander ("salamandra"), according to ancient lore, could live in a burning flame; hence it was often used as a symbol of a lover in the flames of love. 2. The phoenix ("fénix") was a mythical bird who, every hundred years, would ignite itself in its nest and be consumed by fanning the flames with its wings. A new phoenix was born from a worm in the ashes.

[21] Tono humano   ([Juan de] Navas)

Estribillo

Puesto que baja el amor a la tierra
de cándidos cisnes batiendo las alas,
sudando el calor que en el pecho se enciende
deshilen los ojos océanos de agua.

Since love is going down to the earth,
as white swans beating their wings,
sweating the heat that is fired up in the heart,
let the eyes stream oceans of water.

Coplas

1. Pues hoy la fortuna se sube a su esfera,
   que son los vagos palacios del viento,
   despedidas las llamas del alma,
   lloren los ojos centellas de fuego.

2. A herir de Eritrea[1] y de Cintia[2] los pechos
   la hebra florida fecunda mi planta,
   pues para hacerlos en todo infelices
   hacer queridos los jóvenes basta.

3. Al aire me subo a encender un peligro
   porque los hombres, errados al verlo,
   por castigo lo tengan y no por desdicha
   y mi envidia parezca influjo del cielo.

Since fortune is rising today to her sphere,
which is in the vague palaces of the wind,
as the flames of the soul are emitted,
let the eyes weep sparks of fire.

To wound the hearts of Eritrea and Cintia,
my step brings forth the lush filament;
and in order to make them completely unhappy,
it is sufficient to make youth beloved.

I rise into the air to stir up a danger
so that men, mistaken upon seeing it,
will think it a punishment and not a misfortune,
and my envy will seem to be caused by the heavens.

Source: Segovia, Cathedral Archive.
Music: M. 9, voice, note 3 is two tied sixteenth-notes. M. 10, voice, fermata lacking. M. 19, continuo, note 4 is an eighth-note.
Text: Parts of this poem are very difficult to interpret, possibly because of errors in the copy. It seems that the goddess of love speaks in the *coplas*. It is the only poem in this edition that has a fixed accent pattern, being in *arte mayor* with each line consisting of four amphibrachic feet. 1. Source has "eric trea" instead of "Eritrea" (the name of a sibyl). 2. Source has "cintria" instead of "Cintia" (a name associated with Diana and, hence, chastity).

[22] Solo humano   (Anonymous)

Estribillo

Niña, si encontrares[1]
durmiendo a Cupido,
si velar no quieres,[2]
déjale[3] dormido.

Maiden, if you find
Cupid sleeping and you do not
want to suffer from insomnia,
let him sleep.

Coplas

1. Durmiendo estaba una tarde
   en las flores Cupidillo,
   que se duerme fácilmente
   quien es ciego y quien es niño.

2. No está siempre Amor despierto;
   tal vez suele conducirlo
   la mudanza y el cansancio
   al letargo del olvido.

3. Y una zagaleja[4] libre
   de su amoroso dominio
   no queriendo querer nunca[5]
   quiso despertarle y quiso.

Little Cupid was sleeping
one afternoon among the flowers,
for he who is blind and a child
easily falls asleep.

Love is not always awake;
perhaps fickleness and fatigue
often lead him
to the drowsiness of oblivion.

A shepherd girl free
from his amorous power,
never wanting to fall in love,
wanted to wake him, and she fell in love.

Source: Venice, Biblioteca Nazionale Marciana, Mus. MS H.IV, 470 (= 9994) (Cantarini), fols. 9ᵛ–11ᵛ.
Music: The rhythmic unit in the source is equivalent to $\frac{9}{8}$ syncopated frequently. M. 35, voice, note 1 is missing in source.
Text: 1. Source spells this word "encantrares." 2. This line is "si velando quieres" (= if staying awake you want) in source. 3. This word is spelled "desale" in the source. 4. Source spells this word "zagalesa." 5. Source spells this word "nuncia."

[23] Tonada sola con flautas para contralto   (Sebastián Durón)

Estribillo

Corazón, causa tenéis,
si sentís, si suspiráis,
si tembláis, si padecéis,
   pues el Dios a quien teméis
es el que injusto agraváis,
y estrecha cuenta daréis.
   Corazón, causa tenéis,
si sentís, si suspiráis,
si tembláis, si padecéis.

Heart, you have a reason
if you grieve, if you sigh,
if you tremble, if you suffer,
   since the God whom you love
is the one you unjustly wrong,
and you will give an exact rendering.
   Heart, you have a reason
if you grieve, if you sigh,
if you tremble, if you suffer.

Coplas

1.   Si teméis la estrecha cuenta
del severísimo juez,
más del caso es enmendar
que gastar tiempo en temer.
   Si lloráis y padecéis,
corazón, causa tenéis.

If you fear the exact rendering
of the most severe judge,
it is up to you to mend your ways
rather than waste time fearing.
   If you weep and suffer,
heart, you have a reason.

2.   Si padecéis sus pesares,
el medio más digno es,
desengañándoos del mundo,
crucificaros con él.
   Si lloráis y padecéis,
corazón, causa tenéis.

If you suffer his sorrows,
the most dignified remedy
is to retire from the world,
crucify yourself with him.
   If you weep and suffer,
heart, you have a reason.

3.   El verle crucificado
os haga llorar por ver
quan mal vuestra ingratitud
paga tan constante fe.
   Si lloráis y padecéis,
corazón, causa tenéis.

May seeing him crucified
make you weep by seeing
how poorly your ingratitude
repays such constant faith.
   If you weep and suffer,
heart, you have a reason.

4.   Si sentís el propio error,
sentís, corazón, muy bien,
y será eterno vivir
momentáneo padecer.
   Si lloráis y padecéis,
corazón, causa tenéis.

If you grieve for your own mistakes,
you grieve very well, heart,
and this instant of suffering
will be an eternal life.
   If you weep and suffer,
heart, you have a reason.

SOURCE: Transcription made from source in a Spanish archive; present location of the source is unknown.
MUSIC: Mm. 25–26 and 43 (second half)–45, voice, tied notes are single dotted half-note, as final note of section in source.

[24] Tonada humana   (Sebastián Durón)

1.   Pues me pierdo en lo que callo
el desdén de lo que adoro,[1]
   ¡gran bobería,
   capricho loco
fuera por ser callado
   no ser dichoso!
      ¿Gustas?
   Ya soy discreto,
   pues no soy corto.
¿Te enojas? Pues, no quiero.
   Vuelvo a ser bobo.

Since I am losing in my silence
the disdain of that which I adore,
   great stupidity,
   foolish caprice
it would be by being silent
   not to be happy!
      Do you approve?
   Now I am wise,
   since I am not timid.
You become angry? Then I do not love.
   I am becoming an idiot again.

2.	Díla, que no estoy en mí	Say it, for I am in no mood
	de lograr tu desdén solo.	to have your disdain by myself.
	¡Gran bobería,	Great stupidity,
	capricho loco	foolish caprice
	fuera haberme quedado	it would be to have kept
	conmigo propio!	it all to myself!
	¿Gustas?	Do you approve?
	Ya soy discreto,	Now I am wise,
	pues no soy corto.	since I am not timid.
	¿Te enojas? Pues, no quiero.	You become angry? Then I do not love.
	Vuelvo a ser bobo.	I am becoming an idiot again.

SOURCE: Printed in Madrid, n.d.; Segovia, Cathedral Archive, N. 41/28.

MUSIC: M. 3, voice, note 2 is an eighth-note; continuo, note 1 is a quarter-note. M. 18, voice, slur between notes 1 and 2.

TEXT: 1. The poet debates whether to speak out and risk the disdain of his beloved or be quiet and unknown.

[25] Cantada a voz sola al Santísimo y de Pasión   ([Sebastián] Durón)

Recitado

Ay de mí, que el llanto y la tristeza	Woe is me, for weeping and sadness
no, no ablanda mi dureza.	do not soften my rigidity.
Criad, Señor, en mí piedad, usando	Create, my Lord, piety in me, using
un limpio corazón, humilde y blando,	a clean heart, humble and soft,
y para que respiren mis sentidos,	and so that my senses breathe,
dad gozo y alegría a mis oídos.	give pleasure and happiness to my ears.

Aria

1.	Consiga afligido	Let my love, conquered
	mi afecto rendido	and afflicted, gain
	la gracia que el alma	the grace that my soul
	infelice perdió—	unhappily lost—
	afligido, rendido,	afflicted, conquered,
	la gracia que el alma	the grace that my soul
	infelice perdió—	unhappily lost—
	pues nunca el que llega	for never does my God
	llorando y se entrega	despise him who comes
	contrito y humilde	crying and surrenders himself,
	desprecia mi Dios.	with contrition and humility.

2.	Aunque soy indigno,	Even though I am unworthy,
	tu rostro benigno,	my Lord, do not remove
	mi dueño, no apartes	your benign face
	de mi corazón;	from my heart,
	tu rostro benigno,	my Lord, do not remove
	mi dueño, no apartes	your benign face
	de mi corazón;	from my heart,
	ni quites airado	nor take your spirit
	tu espíritu, amado,	haughtily, beloved,
	del alma afligida	from the afflicted heart
	que pide perdón.	that asks for forgiveness.

Recitado

Mas, ¡ay!, que aunque el dolor mi aliento excede,	But woe, for even though the pain exceeds my breath,
nadie el perdón asegurarme puede,	no one can assure me of your forgiveness,
pues sabiendo la causa porque lloro,	since knowing the reason why I weep,
si está borrado mi delito ignoro,	I do not know if my crimes are erased,
y como temerosamente espero,	and as I hope fearfully,
con temor y esperanza vivo y muero.	with fear and hope I live and die.

SOURCE: Guatemala City, Cathedral Archive, MS 259.
MUSIC: M. 1, voice, note 1 has word "Mas" (crossed out) underlaid to it, and note 2 is two eighth-notes with words "ay de" underlaid to them. M. 52, voice, beat 3 is two eighth-notes (b', b').

[26] Cantada al Santísimo con violines   ([Sebastián] Durón)

Estribillo

¡Ay, que me abraso	Oh, how I burn
de amor en la llama!	in the flame of love!
¡Qué dulce violencia!	What sweet violence!
¡Qué tierna regala!¹	What a tender gift!
Celestes incendios	Celestial fires
al pecho motivan,²	ignite the heart
que anhela el tormento,	which desires torment,
que es gloria del alma.	the glory of the soul.

Recitado

O guerra misteriosa	O mysterious war
en la forma gloriosa,	in glorious form,
vivamente contemplo	I contemplate intently,
a quien erige templo,	my soul in anxiety,
ansiosa el alma mía,	him who erects the temple,
remedio de mi ciega fantasía.	remedy of my blind fantasy.

Aria

No deje de arder	Do not let my faithful
mi fiel corazón;	heart cease burning;
será la ocasión	it will be the occasion
de mi merecer—	of my merit—
no, no deje de arder;	do not cease burning;
verá que en su fuego	you will see that in its fire
la dicha halla luego	it soon finds the happiness
de mi padecer.	of my suffering.

Coplas

1. Anime, amor, la llama	Vivify, love, the flame
del celestial incendio,	of the celestial fire.
seré en sus puras alas	I will be on its pure wings
glorioso fénix si renazco al cielo.	a glorious phoenix, if I am reborn to the heavens.
2. Avive la materia	Let the material revive
mi amor y mi deseo,	my love and desire,
prestando mis suspiros	lending my sighs to the air
al aire que voraz anima el fuego.	that fans the fires voraciously.
3. El corazón la ofrenda	My heart will be the offering,
será, pues el primero	since the first heart was the one
fue quien al dueño mío	who opened the doors
franqueó las puertas del humano templo.	of the human temple to my lord.

Grave

Y en tan celestiales	And in such celestial,
divinos incendios,	divine fires,
al suave amoroso	let my breast,
suspiro que exhala,	to the soft amorous
repita mi pecho	sigh that it exhales
su fiel consonancia.	repeat its faithful consonance.

SOURCE: Palencia, Cathedral Archive, MS 50/1.
MUSIC: Mm. 51–53, source has a repeat sign for the voice part of mm. 46–50. M. 81, voice, note 1 is a quarter-note. M. 91, voice, note 1 is a quarter-note. Mm. 94–95, organ, double bar is at end of m. 94. M. 117, continuo, bass figure "2" is

under note 2, not note 1, and note 3 is an eighth-note. M. 122, continuo, note 3 is an eighth-note. Mm. 125–34, voice, organ, and continuo, these parts are barred irregularly in $\frac{3}{4}$, $\frac{3}{8}$, and $\frac{6}{8}$; violins are barred in $\frac{6}{8}$. M. 134, all parts except continuo, source gives "Al principio" or "Finis de principio," which has been assumed to mean *D.C. Estribillo*.

TEXT: 1. Given here as in the source, even though one would expect the masculine noun *regalo;* the assonance a/a is needed for the rhyme. 2. Given here as in the source, even though "motivan" does not rhyme.

[27] Solo humano   ([Juan de Lima] Serqueira)

Estribillo

Quería Cupido, traidor y halagüeño, herir con sus flechas de Anarda los ceños, pero ella decía, burlando su intento: ¡Ay, el hombre! ¡Ay, qué horror! ¡Ay, qué miedo! Rendir mi dureza. ¡Nada menos que eso!	Cupid, treasonous and attractive, wanted to wound with his arrows the scowl of Anarda, but she said, mocking his effort: Ay, the man! What a horror! Ay, what fear! Surrender my firmness. Nothing less than that!

Coplas

1.
Quería el tirano rapaz, ceguezuelo, que en mí la beldad, que nació a ser hechizo, parase en ser riesgo. ¡Ay, el hombre! ¡Ay, qué horror! ¡Ay, qué miedo! Rendir mi dureza. ¡Nada menos que eso!	The tyrant, young, blind, wanted in me my beauty, which was born to bewitch, to end up a risk. Ay, the man! What a horror! Ay, what fear! Surrender my firmness. Nothing less than that!

2.
Quería en mis ojos, mirando el incendio que a la ira sopla el volcán, me tocasen las chispas del fuego. ¡Ay, el hombre¡ ¡Ay, qué horror! ¡Ay, qué miedo! Que me armé yo misma. ¡Nada menos que eso!	He wanted my eyes, looking at the holocaust which in its wrath the volcano breathes forth, to feel the sparks of the fire. Ay, the man! What a horror! Ay, what fear! That I armed myself. Nothing less than that!

3.
Quería que al mayo fértil de mi ceño (le usurpé el verdor) la traición de un influjo entrase de enero. ¡Ay, el hombre! ¡Ay, qué horror! ¡Ay, qué miedo! Marchitan desdenes. ¡Nada menos que eso!	He wanted the treason of a sudden influx of January to enter into the fertile May (from which I stole the green) of my frown. Ay, the man! What a horror! Ay, what fear! Rejection withers. Nothing less than that!

4.
Querrá al fin que de mi estrago mesmo naciese el quedarle la gloria del tiempo y a mí el escarmiento. ¡Ay, el hombre! ¡Ay, qué horror! ¡Ay, qué miedo! Triunfar de quien rinde. ¡Nada menos que eso!	He will want in the end my very destruction to serve to make him the glory of all time and me the moral example. Ay, the man! What a horror! Ay, what fear! To triumph over the conquered. Nothing less than that!

SOURCE: Segovia, Cathedral Archive.
MUSIC: M. 11, continuo, note 1 does not have a dot. M. 23, continuo, note 3 does not have a dot.

[28] Solo humano   ([Juan de Lima] Serqueira)

Estribillo

Ay, Leonida,
si mis quejas, mis suspiros
son lisonjas de tus ceños,
de mis penas son testigos.
    El aire se queja
de verse oprimido
con el embarazo
de tantos gemidos. ˙
	Ah, Leonida,
	if my laments, my sighs,
	are praises of your frowns,
	they are witnesses of my sufferings.
	    The air complains
	about seeing itself oppressed
	with the weight
	of so many laments.

Coplas

1.   No hago cargo a tu belleza
de mi robado albedrío,
que no es culpa de tus ojos
el haberme yo perdido.

I do not accuse your beauty
of my stolen will,
for it is not the fault of your eyes
that I became lost.

2.   Ya podré yo contentarme
con que tu desdén esquivo;
no mude el nombre a esta ofrenda
y me la llame delito.

Now I will be able to please myself,
that I avoid your disdain;
do not change the name of suffering
and call it a sin in me.

3.   Pártase en los dos el coste
de este amante sacrificio,
y pues pongo en el alma
por riqueza lo benigno.

Let the cost of this lover's sacrifice
be split in two,
and then I will place in my soul
the benign as wealth.

SOURCE: Segovia, Cathedral Archive.

[29] Tono humano solo   ([Juan de Lima] Serqueira)

Estribillo

Todo es amor: el arroyo, la estrella y la flor; aprende, Tirsi bella, de la flor, el arroyo y la estrella, y verás tu rigor; que nada es desdén; que todo es amor: el arroyo, la estrella, la flor, y llorando, ardiendo, espirando, en cristal, en incendio, en olor, el arroyo, la estrella y la flor; nada es desdén; todo es amor: el arroyo, llorando en cristal, en incendios ardiendo la estrella y la flor espirando en olor. Todo es amor: llorando el arroyo, ardiendo la estrella, espirando la flor, en cristal, en incendio, en olor. Todo es amor: el arroyo, la estrella, la flor.	Everything is love: the stream, the star, and the flower; learn, beautiful Tirsi, from the flower, the stream, and the star, and you will see your cruelty; for nothing is disdain; everything is love: the stream, the star, the flower, and weeping, burning, exhaling, in crystal, in fire, in scent, the stream, the star, and the flower; nothing is disdain; everything is love: the stream, weeping in crystal, in fire, the star burning, and the flower, exhaling scent. Everything is love: the stream weeping, the star burning, the flower exhaling, in crystal, in fire, in scent. Everything is love: the stream, the star, the flower.

Coplas

1. Aquel arroyuelo,
    galán de las selvas,
    sus troncos inunda
    y sus flores riega,
    y amante celebra
    con llanto de cristal
    de amor las penas.

    That small stream,
    suitor of the forests,
    floods its trees
    and waters its flowers,
    and as a lover celebrates
    with the weeping of water
    the suffering of love.

2. Rayos esparciendo,
    la amorosa estrella
    a voces ardientes
    la aurora despierta,
    y amante celebra
    con ecos de esplendor
    de amor las penas.

    The amorous star
    spreading rays
    awakens the dawn
    with ardent voices,
    and as a lover celebrates
    with echoes of splendor
    the suffering of love.

3. La flor cariñosa
    al sol galantea,
    ardiendo sus rayos
    en dichosa hoguera,
    y amante celebra
    con suspiros de olor
    de amor las penas.

    The endearing flower
    courts the sun,
    its rays burning
    in a happy configuration,
    and as a lover celebrates
    with scented sighs
    the suffering of love.

4. Ama, ingrata Tirsi,
    pues a amor te invoco,
    amando el arroyo,
    la flor y la estrella,
    que amantes celebran
    en cristal, luz y olor
    de amor las penas.

    Love, ungrateful Tirsi,
    for I call you to love,
    with the steam, the flower,
    and the star loving,
    who as lovers celebrate
    in crystal, light, and scent
    the sufferings of love.

SOURCE: Barcelona, Biblioteca Central, Music MS 775/79.
EDITION: Felipe Pedrell, *Teatro lírico español*, 4–5:50–52.
MUSIC: It would seem unlikely that the *estribillo* should be repeated between each of the *coplas*, not only because of its length, but also because each *copla* has its own refrain. Mm. 69–70, continuo, source gives only a single whole-note.

[30] Cantada humana ([Juan de Lima] Serqueira)

Estribillo

O corazón amante,
o cómo el alma siente
aquel dolor constante[1]
que halaga dulcemente
cuando fallezco yo.
Nunca falte herida
que a una dichosa vida
que halaga dulcemente
su espíritu flamante
cuando fallezco yo.

Oh, loving heart,
oh, how the soul feels
that constant pain
which sweetly flatters
when I am dying.
Never let a happy life
want for a wound
that sweetly flatters
its flaming spirit
when I am dying.

Recitado

Fili, si este suspiro,
esta ansia, esta fineza
alguna seña deja
a tu piedad fiada,
vaya mi vida al aire encomendada,
mas, ¡ay!, que si mi voz lleva mi acento,
el viento llevará lo que es del viento.

Phyllis, if this sigh,
this anxiety, this favor,
leaves a mark
trusting your mercy,
let my life go entrusted to the air,
but, oh, if my voice carries my accent,
the wind will carry away that which belongs to the wind.

Aria

Ni tú puedes dejar,
Fili hermosa,
de ser rigurosa,
ingrata y cruel.

    Ni yo puedo dejar
el empeño de amar
ese ceño
y en ansia dichosa
morirme por él.

And you cannot,
beautiful Phyllis,
keep from being harsh,
ungrateful, and cruel.

    Nor can I leave
the persistence of loving
that frown,
and in happy anxiety
die for it.

SOURCE: Madrid, Biblioteca Nacional, Music MS M. 2618, "P[adre] Fr[ay] Anselmo de Lera, Predicador de S[u] M[a-jestad] en S[an] Martin: Cantadas a lo humano con accompañamiento de violín y oboe—1737—Dd. 215," pp. 58–60.

MUSIC: Only the vocal part survives; the continuo, violin, and oboe parts have been reconstructed by the editor (see The Edition). M. 7, voice, note 1 is two tied half-notes. M. 12, voice, notes 7 and 8 are quarter-notes. M. 13, voice, notes 1–3 are slurred. M. 15, voice, note 4 is a quarter-note. M. 21, voice, source has an extra eighth-note (c"), omitted here. M. 30, voice, note 5 is lacking. M. 55, voice, notes 1 and 2 are in ligature. M. 71, voice, note 3 is a quarter-note. M. 78, voice, note 4 is a dotted eighth. M. 93, voice, note 1 has no dot.

TEXT: 1. Source has "dolor amante" with word "constante" written below the "amante" in a different hand; the editor has accepted what seems to be a correction.

[31] Cantada humana   ([Juan de Lima] Serqueira)

Recitado

En la ribera verde
del patrio Manzanares,[1]
así Marcelo canta
a su adorado bien
quejas amantes.[2]

On the green bank
of his native Manzanares,
Marcelo thus sings
to his adored beloved
a lover's complaint.

Aria

Máteme infiel tu poder,
mas no acabe de morir.
No porque quiero vivir,
sino por más padecer,
que muerto podré querer
pero no podré sentir.
Máteme infiel tu poder,
mas no acabe de morir.

Let your power ungratefully kill me,
but don't let me die.
Not because I want to live,
but in order to suffer more;
for dead I will be able to love,
but I will not be able to feel.
Let your power ungratefully kill me,
but don't let me die.

Recitado

Belisa, yo obstinado he de adorarte,
aunque te pierda mi infelice suerte,
pues por el interés de no perderte,
no he de dejar el mérito de amarte.
Pues si del destino la inflüencia[3]
me diere por castigo el de la ausencia,
advierte que al aliento de un suspiro
no hay segura distancia en el[4] retiro.

Belisa, I stubbornly must love you,
even though I lose you unluckily,
since in hope of not losing you,
I must not quit loving you.
But if the influence of destiny
gives me the punishment of absence,
be warned that for the breath of a sigh
there is no safe distance in retreat.

Aria

Viva alegre mi contento;
ame fiel mi corazón.
    Que el aliento
por tormento
tan violento

May my happiness live contentedly;
may my heart love faithfully.
    Since the breath
in such violent
torture

no es bien,
deje la pasión.
    Viva alegre mi contento;
ame fiel mi corazón.

Fuga

    Aguas que corréis,
aves que voláis,
cielos que giráis,
auras que mecéis,
corred, volad,
girad, meced,
y el dulce tormento
de amor explicad
al bello motivo
de mi padecer.

is not good,
reliquish passion.
    May my happiness live contentedly;
may my heart love faithfully.

    Waters that flow,
birds that fly,
heavens that turn,
breezes that sway,
flow, fly,
turn, sway,
and explain the sweet
torture of love
to the pretty reason
of my suffering.

SOURCE: Madrid, Biblioteca Nacional, Music MS M. 2816, "P[adre] Fr[ay] Anselmo de Lera, Predicador de S[u] M[a-jestad] en S[an] Martin: Cantadas a lo humano con acompañamiento de violín y oboe—1737—Dd. 215," pp. 6–9.

MUSIC: Only the vocal part survives; the continuo, violin, and oboe parts have been reconstructed by the editor (see The Edition). M. 54, voice, note 3 is a quarter-note. Mm. 56 and 122, voice, although the source has no *D.C.* indication, the intention to do so seems clear from the music. M. 59, voice, note 4 has no dot. M. 88, voice, notes 1 and 4 have no dots. M. 126, voice, note 9 is a half-note. M. 133, voice, source has four quarter-notes grouped by a slur.

TEXT: 1. Manzanares is a river that runs through Madrid. 2. Another hand has added "del alma" (= of the soul), perhaps as an alternate reading, at the end of this line. 3. This line is short by two syllables; source seems to have another "a" at the end of the line. 4. The word "el" has been editorially added for correct poetic scansion.

Index of First Lines

In addition to listing the first lines of all the songs, this Index includes the incipits of the *estribillos* that do not precede the *coplas* and the incipits of metrically different pieces embedded in other songs.

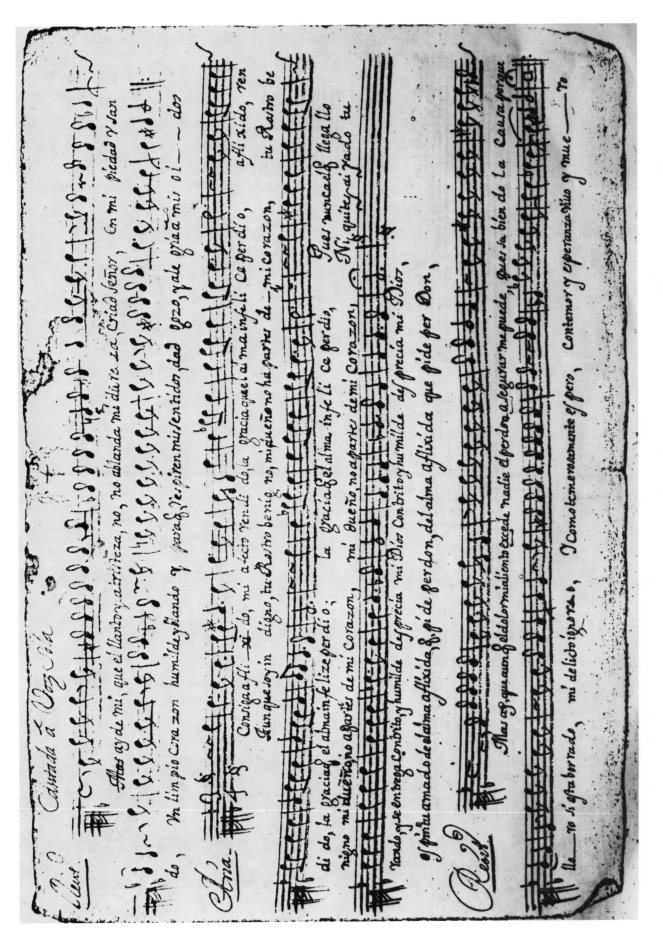

Plate I. [Sebastián] Durón, "Cantada a voz sola" (no. 25), voice part.
(Guatemala City, Cathedral Archive, MS 259. Source size: 31 cm. x 21.5 cm.)

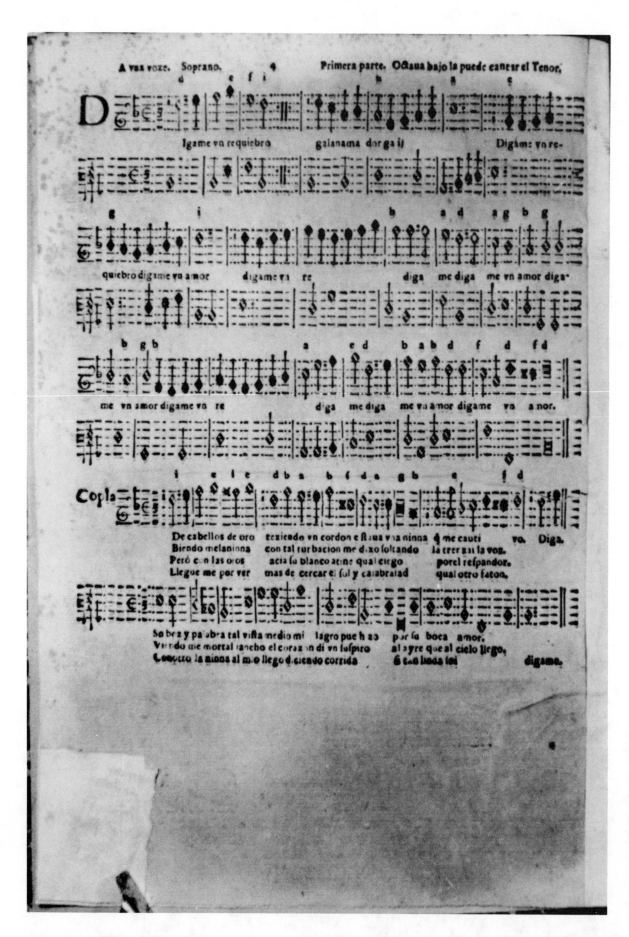

Plate II. Juan Aranies, "Tono humano" (no. 4), from *Libro segundo de tonos y villancicos* (Rome, 1624), no. 2. (Bologna, Civico Museo, V101)

SPANISH ART SONG
IN THE
SEVENTEENTH CENTURY

[1] Air

Anonymous

1. De- cid có- mo pue- de ser, o- jos, que_es- tan- do mi- ran- do, do,
2. De- cid, o- jos, con en- ga- ño vi- vís con mu-cho con- ten- to, to,
3. Y a- sí pen-sáis me_ re- cer el bien que_es- téis de- se- an- do: do:
4. O qué bien sa- béis fin- gir, mos-tran- do te- ner so- sie- go, go,
5. Su- je- taos a pa- de- cer lo que pren-dis-tes mi- ran- do: do:

a- le- gres, a- le- gres es- téis pe- nan- do y
a- có- mo te- néis, a- có- mo te- néis su- fri- mien- to pa y
a- si_en____ vien- do, si_en____ vien- do dais a sen- tir_____ que_a y
a- le- gres, a- le- gres es- téis pe- nan- do y

tris- tes mos- tréis pla- cer, y tris- tes mos- tréis pla- cer. cer.
- ra pa- sar tan- tos da- ños, pa- ra pa- sar tan- tos da- ños. da- ños.
tris- tes mos- tréis pla- cer, y tris- tes mos- tréis pla- cer. cer.
- bra- sáis en vi- vo fue- go, que_a- bra- sáis en vi- vo fue- go. fue- go.
tris- tes mos- tréis pla- cer, y tris- tes mos- tréis pla- cer. cer.

Each of the source ornaments (★ ∴) could be interpreted as a mordent, a trill, or a vibrato.

[2] Air

Gabriel Bataille

1. Si su- fro por ____ ti, mo- re- na, mu- cho me pla- ce
2. ¿Qué te sir- ve, ____ cruel A- mor, ____ tor- men- tar- me con
3. El mal que me ha- ces sen- tir, ____ con- ten- to me ha- ce
4. Si ja- más la ol- vi- da- ré ____ el tiem- po que pa-

mi pe- na, pues van tus o- jos mi- ran- do, al mis- mo sol ad- mi- ran- do.
do- lor?, ____ pues que me pla- ce la pe- na que su- fro por mi mo- re- na.
vi- vir, ____ pues yo me huel- go en la pe- na que su- fro por mi mo- re- na.
-sa- ré, ____ con- ti- no ha- ga la pe- na pues dé- ja- me mi mo- re- na.

[3] Pasacalle: La folie

[Henri] de Bailly

1. Yo
2. Sir-

The source ornament (★) could be interpreted as a mordent, a trill, or a vibrato.

soy la lo- cu- ra,____ la que so- la in- fun- do pla- cer, pla-
-ven a mi nom- bre____ to- dos mu- cho o po- co, y no, y

-cer y dul- zu- ra y con- ten- se to al mun- do, do.____
no, no hay hom- bre que pien- se ser lo- co, co.____

[4] [Tono humano]

Juan Aranies

Estribillo

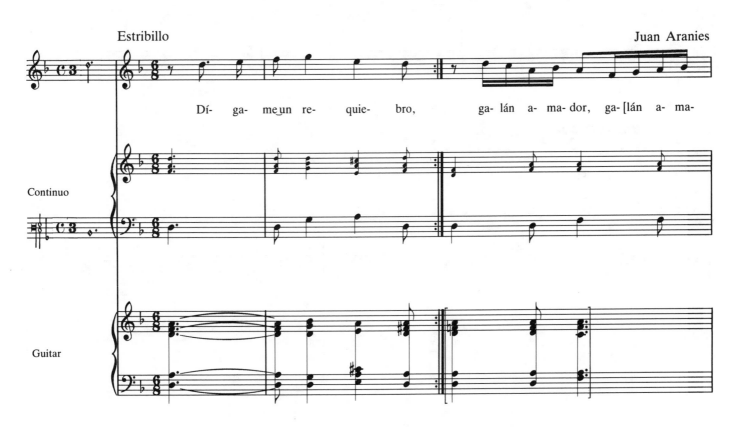

Dí- ga me un re- quie- bro, ga- lán a- ma- dor, ga- [lán a- ma-

Continuo

Guitar

- dor;] dí- ga-me un re- quie-bro; dí- ga-me un a- mor, dí- ga-me un re-[quie-bro; dí- ga-me un a-

- mor,] dí- ga- me, dí- ga- me un a- mor, dí- ga- me un a- mor, dí- ga- me un re-

- [quie-bro; dí-ga-me un a- mor,] dí- ga- me, dí- ga-me un a- mor, dí- ga- me un a- mor.

Fine

attacca

Coplas

[D.C. Estribillo after coplas 1 and 7]

*F-sharp when guitar accompanies; f-natural when continuo accompanies.

[5] Folías

Coplas

Luis de Briceño

Guitar

1. Vo- la- ba la pa- lo- mi- ta por en-ci- ma del ver-de li- món,

con las a- las _ a- par- ta las _ ra-mas, con el pi- co lle- va ___ la flor.

2. A- rro- jó- me las man- za- ne- tas por en-ci- ma del man-za-

-nar; a- rro- jó- me-las y a- rro- jé- se- las y tor- nó-me- las _ [a]a- rro- jar.

*Music for the voice has been reconstructed by the editor.

3. Si ja- más duer-men mis __ o- jos, ma- dre __ mí- a, ¿qué ha- rán?,

que co- mo a-mor los des- ve- la, pien-so que se mo- ri- rán. 4. Quien

di- jo __ muer- te al a- mor __ li- bre __ de pe- sa- res e- ra;

me- jor di- je- ra __ do- lor y más na- tu- ral __ le fue- ra. 5. U- na

mo- ra en mí e- na- mo- ra, por __ ser __ mo- ra de na- ción,

8

mas no es mo- ra____ pues____ que mo- ra den- tro de mi___ co- ra- zón.

[6] Solo al Santísimo

Estribillo

Matías Veana

Ay,___ a- mor, ay, ay,___ a- mor, qué dul- ce ti-

-ra- no te con- tem- plo hoy, pues su- je- tas, [pues su-

-je- tas] a los más re- bel- des con __ do- ra- dos____

attacca

10

Coplas

1. En-   tre ___   dul-   ces   de-   li-   quios   de_un   al-   ma,   que_a-   fec-   tos   res-ros
2. ¿Has-   ta ___   cuán-   do,   o_Es-   po-   so,   de -   cías   en-   tre_obs-   cu-ros
3. O ___   si ___   ros-   tro   a   ros-   tro   te   vie-   se,   o   pe-   no-   sa_au-me
4. De-   rri-   bad, ___   mi_a-   ma-   do,   la   cár-   cel   que_a-   sí   me   de-me
5. Si_a-   blan-   do   y_a-   ten-   do   tus   fi-   ne-   zas,   fle-   chad-   me
6. Bas-   te, ___   bas-   te,   se-   ñor   de   dul-   zu-   ras,   que_es   gran-   de   la_he-

30

- pi-   ra   de_a-   man-   te   pa-   sión,   se ___   per-   ci-   ben   los   ai-   res   gus-
- ve-   los   he   de   ver   tu_a-   mor?,   y ___   la   ci-   te-   la   que_o-   cul-   ta_el   e-
- sen-   cia,   o   fuer-   te   do-   lor,   pues   vio-   ra   len-   ta_mi   al-   ma   se
- tie-   ne can-   sa-   da_y   sin   voz,   que _   la ___   muer-   te   de   tan   dul-   ce
- sua-   ve   el   maś   fuer-   te_ar-   pón,   pa-   ra ___   ir   a_e-   se_al-   cá-   zar   ce-
- ri-   da   y   más   el   ar-   dor,   y ___   no_hay ___   fuer-   za   que   re-   sis-   tir

- to-   sos,   e-   fec-   tos   gus-   to-   [sos]   que   cau-   sa   la_u-   nión.
- nig-   ma   no   e-   ras-   tre   las   ca-   se-   a   des-   po-   jo   del   sol.
- ha-   lla   en-   tre   las   ca-   de-   nas   de_hu-   ma-   na   pa-   sión.
- les-   te,   glo-   rio-   so   pa-   la-   cio,   di-   vi-   na   re-   gión.
- ti-   ro   es   vi-   da   per-   pe-   tua   de   mi   co-   ra-   zón.
- pue-   da_a_im-   pul-   sos   di-   vi-   nos   tal   lla-   ma   ma-   yor.

Ay,

35

ay,   ay, ___   a-   mor.   ay,   ay,   ay, ___   a-   mor.

[7] Solo al Sacramento

José Asturiano

Estribillo

Cé- fi-ros blan-dos, lí- qui-das fuen-tes, ta, que des-

-can- sa, ta,___ que se duer-me a las fa- ti- gas de mis des-

-de- nes fie- ro Cu- pi- do— no le des- pier- ten.

Cé- fi- ros blan- dos, lí- qui- das fuen- tes.

attacca

Coplas

1. Mú- si- cas ce- les- tes vo- ces   cé- fi- ros pu- lan y sue- nen;
2. Má- xi-mo em- pe- ño la ci- fra,   tér- mi- no la o- cul- ta bre- ve,
3. Pró- vi-do a- mor co- mo sa- bio   púr- pu- ra pre- cio- sa vier- te,
4. Só- li- da pie- dra la ba- sa,   fá- bri-ca y mu- ro tan fuer- te,
5. Án- ge- les pu- ros y hom- bres   á- gui- las a su luz vue- len;

pá- ja- ros se oi- gan qué dul- ces   cán- ti- cos
mú- si- co a- mor, blan- do cis- ne,   cán- di- do ex-
tó- si- go que ar- mo- ni- za al ma- lo,   bá- cu- lo
ú- ni- ca o- fre- ce tu o- bra   dó- ri- co al
Hér- cu- les a- man- tes triun- fen;   ví- bo- ras

6   6

mís- ti- cos fuer- tes.   Mú- si- cas vo- ces,   cé- fi- ros sue- nen,
-tá- ti- co fé- nix.   Má- xi- ma ci- fra,   tér- mi- no bre- ve,
que al- can- za al dé- bil.   Pró- vi- do sa- bio   púr- pu- ra vier- te,
al- ma su al- ber- gue.   Só- li- da ba- sa,   fá- bri- ca fuer- te,
en can- tos hue- llen.   Án- ge- les y hom- bres,   á- gui- las vue- len,

        ♯   6   6   6   ♯ 6 ♯
                                                3♭

pá- ja- ros dul- ces,   cán- ti- cos fuer- tes.
mú- si- co cis- ne,   cán- di- do fé- nix.
tó- si- go al ma- lo,   bá- cu- lo al dé- bil.
ú- ni- ca o- bra,   dó- ri- co al ber- gue.
Hér- cu- les triun- fen,   ví- bo- ras hue- llen.

        6   6   ♯   6   ♯ 6 ♯
                                          3♭

[8] Solo al Santísimo

Estribillo

[Diego de or José de] Cásseda

14

-dien-cia sin o- jos, trai- ga ___ la fe, trai- ga, ___ trai- ga la fe, la o-be-dien-cia sin

o- jos, la o-be-dien- cia sin o- jos trai- ga ___ la fe, trai- ga ___ la

fe, trai- ga ___ la fe, trai- ga ___ la fe.

Fine

attacca

Coplas

1. En el so- lio de un a- bril, ___ el rey de la ma- je-
2. Ce- le- brar qui- so las cor- tes en es-ta es- tan- cia re-
3. Su san-gre y car- ne pro- po- ne pa- ra re- me-dio e- fi-
4. Es el dí- a de las cor- tes al Cor- pus ya quien le-
5. Rin- den hu- mil-de ho- me- na- je, pe- ro con ga- nan- cia
6. El ser- vi- cio que le ha- cen es a- mor; la vo- lun-
7. Ca- da ley de su fi- ne- za pro- di- gio a pas- cuas se- no
8. A dos fue- ros la ob- ser- van- cia pro- se ha de re- du- cir no
9. Gran- des mer- ce- des pro- me- te rey que u- só tan- to ve-

D.C. Estribillo

[9] Tono humano

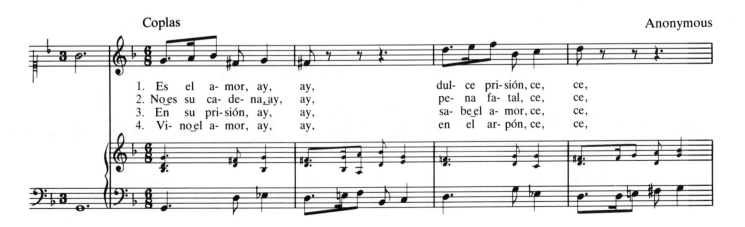

Coplas

Anonymous

1. Es el a- mor, ay, ay,   dul- ce pri- sión, ce,   ce,
2. No es su ca- de- na, ay, ay,   pe- na fa- tal, ce,   ce,
3. En su pri- sión, ay, ay,   sa- be el a- mor, ce,   ce,
4. Vi- no el a- mor, ay, ay,   en el ar- pón, ce,   ce,

que al co- ra- zón, ta, ta, le ha-ce fe- liz, que, que, pues en a- man-te
que es su ri- gor, ta, ta, el ha- la- gar, que, que, pues en su ha- la- go
al pa- de- cer, ta, ta, dar el su- frir, que, que, pues en el pa- de-
lo- gra el ren- dir, ta, ta, to- do bla-són, que, que, pues en su es- qui-

ley, se mi-ra el a- mor en el mis-mo ar-der,
ves, se mi-ra el su-frir por fe- liz pla-cer,
-cer, se mi-ra el sen- tir co-mo dul-ce ley, ay, ay, ay,
-vez, se mi-ra el ren-dir sin que- rer que- rer,

ce, ce, ce, ta, ta, ta, que, que, que,

ay, ay, ce, ce, ta, ta, que, que.

[10] Solo a la vida humana

Estribillo

Anonymous

Es- ta_es la jus- ti- cia que man- da_ha- cer a- mor po- de-

-ro- so, de las al- mas rey, a_un hom- bre_in- fe-

-li- ce, a_un hom- [bre_in- fe- li- ce] por- que qui- so bien.

Fine

attacca

Coplas

1. Man- da que_el ri- gor   le sa-   que de la
2. Man- da que crü- el   mi- nis-   tro con ri-
3. Man- da que_en tris- tes   me- mo-   rias de_es- te_a-
4. Man- da que_en la re-   vis-   ta no_a- guar-
5. Man- da_en fin a la des- di-   cha de_a- mor

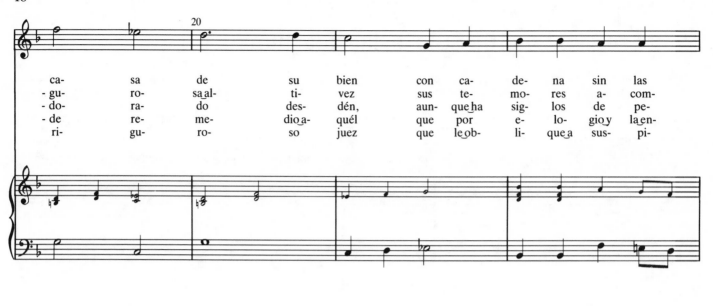

ca- sa de su bien con ca- de- na sin las
gu- ro- sa al- ti- vez sus te- mo- res a- com-
do- ra- do me- dio a- quél que por e- lo- gio y la en-
ri- gu- ro- so juez que le ob- li- que a sus- pi-

D.C. Estribillo

so- gas y con gri- llos en los pies.
pa- ñe- res, al su- pli- cio de u- na fe.
sa- vi- dia con- de- na- do em- bis- ta- fe.
rar, a mo- rir ya pa- de- cer.

[11] Tonada sola

Estribillo   José Marín

A- guas de Man- za- na- res, que a- le- gres co- rréis, que a- le- gres co- rréis, _ que a- le-

-gres, _____ a- le - gres co- rréis, ¿quién pen- sa- ra tan tris- te,

¿quién [pen- sa- ra tan tris- te] que os vol- vie- ra a ver?, ¿quién pen- sa- ra tan

tris- te, ¿quién [pen- sa- ra tan tris- te] que os vol- vie- ra a

ver?, que os [vol- vie- ra a ver?,] que os vol- vie- ra os vol- vie- ra a ver?

Cuan- do me par- tí, cuan- do me par- tí de vues- tros cris-
Y hoy vuel- vo sin mí, y hoy vuel- vo sin mí con nue- va pa-

Fine

attacca

Coplas

-ta- les, de au-sen- cia los ma- les a- man- te sen- tí, a- man- te sen- tí.
-sión, __ fir- me en la a- fi- ción, __ mu- da- ble en la fe, mu- da- ble en la fe.

1. De e- li- gan- te Guad- a- rra- - ma pi- sa- za- ba la fren- te he- la- do, cuan- do a las
2. Des- he- cha en vi- drios la nie- - ve, pi- go- za- ban ya los pe- ñas- cos, de la pri-
3. Ba- ja- ban des- de las cum- - bres los a- rro- yos de- sa- ta- dos a guar- ne-
4. Tris- te ba- la- ba el pas- tor, _____ cuan- do __ se a- le- gra- ban __ tan- tos, por- que no ha-
5. Y des- cu- brien- do en- tre flo- - res de Man- za- na- res los ____ cam- pos, a sus a-

puer- tas de a- bril _____ es- ta va- lla
-sión del in- vier- no la _____ li- ber- tad, _____
-cer con al- jó- far las ____ nue- vas ga-
-cer lo que to- dos es ____ pa- sión, _____
-guas sus tris- te- zas a- sí les di-

man- dó, es- ta _____ va- lla man- dó, el a- ño.
_ la li- ber- tad _____ del ve- ra- no.
- las, las nue- vas _____ ga - las del pra- do.
_ es pa- sión _____ de un _____ des- di- cha- do.
- jo, a- sí _____ les _____ di - jo can- tan- do:

[12] Pasacalle del 5° tono de 3 para el tono

Coplas

José Marín

1. Diz que e- ra co- mo u- na nie- ve, Ma- ri- ca, la ___ de Ber- lin- ches, y
2. E- ra Ma- ri- ca en su al- de- a, a la que in- ven- tó ___ los es- quin- ces, y
3. Lle- gó Be- ni- to de fue- ra, za- gal de po- cos a- bri- les, muy
4. De es- te co- ra- zón se pa- ga por- que tal vez _ lo que e- li- gen las
5. Con és- te quie- re ca- sar- se pa- ra que na- die la en vi- die, a-
6. Pa- ra la be- ca de es- po- so le ha- ce prue- bas _ de a- pa- ci- ble, pues

Guitar

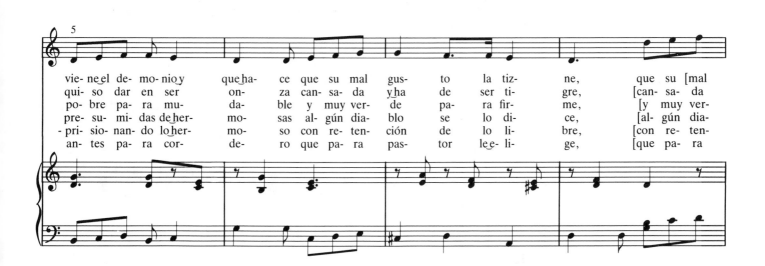

5

vie- ne el de- mo- nio y que ha- ce que su mal gus- to la ti- zne, que su [mal
qui- so dar en ser on- za can- sa- da y ha de ser ti- gre, [can- sa- da
po- bre pa- ra mu- da- ble y muy ver- de pa- fir- me, [y muy ver-
pre- su- mi- das de her- mo- sas al- gún dia- blo se lo di- ce, [al- gún dia-
- pri- sio- nan- do lo her- mo- so con re- ten- ción de lo li- bre, [con re- ten-
an- tes pa- ra cor- de- ro que pa- ra pas- tor le e- li- ge, [que pa- ra

22

gus-   to   la tiz-   ne,]   que su   mal   gus-   to   la tiz-   ne,
y ha   de   ser ti-   gre,   can- sa-   da   y ha   de   ser ti-   gre,]
-de   pa-   ra fir-   me,   y muy   ver-   de   pa-   ra fir-   me,]
-blo   se   lo di-   ce,   al- gún   dia-   blo   se   lo di-   ce,]
-ción   de   lo li-   bre,   con, re-   ten-   ción   de   lo li-   bre,]
pas-   tor   le e-li-   ge,   que pa-   ra   pas-   tor   le e-li-   ge,]

Estribillo

por- que a to- dos di- ce,   por- que a to- dos di- ce

que es pa- ra e- lla, que es pa- ra e- lla el pe- or nin- gu- no,

el me- jor cual- quie- ra,   el me- jor cual- quie- ra.

[13] Pasacalle del 3° tono de 3 para este tono

José Marín

No sé yo có-mo es, no sé yo có-mo es, que quie-ro y no quie-ro y qui- sie-ra que- rer, no

quie-ro y qui- sie-ra que- rer, no sé yo có- mo es, no sé yo có- mo es, que quie-ro y no

quie-ro y qui- sie-ra que- rer, no quie-ro y qui- sie-ra que- rer, no quie-ro y qui- sie-ra que-

- rer, no quie-ro y qui- sie-ra que- rer.

Fine

attacca

Coplas

1. Yo sien-to un no sé que di-ga an- sio- so de he- lar y ar- der   que con él no a-cier-to a es-
2. U- na a- ten- ción des- cui- da- da, un te- mor que ig- no- ra ley   un sa- cri- fi- cio sin
3. Un es- cu- char,___ un oir,___ sin so- bre- sal- to el des- dén,   ha- cer cui- da- do el des-
4. ¿Qué de- sa- li- ña- da fle- cha a- brió el co- ra- zón cru- el,   que me ha- la- ga sien- do
5. Mi- ro sin o- dio mi cul- pa, y con o- dio al- gu- na vez   hu- yo el pe- li- gro y lo

- tar   y no pue-do es- tar sin él,   y no pue-do es- tar sin él;
cul- to,   y u- na a- do- ra- ción sin fe,   y u- na a- do- ra- ción sin fe;
- cui- do   y a du- dar pa- ra cre- er,   y a du- dar pa- ra cre- er; no sé
mal   y a tor- men- ta sien-do bien?,   y a tor- men- ta sien-do bien?,
bus- co,   y só- lo lle- go a en- ten- der,   y só- lo lle- go a en- ten- der:

D.C. Estribillo dal segno 𝄌

yo có- mo es, no sé yo có- mo es._____

[14] Solo a nuestra Señora

Tenor · Estribillo · Juan Hidalgo

Lu- ce- ros _ y _ flo- res, ar- ded y _ lu- cid, al ver u- na au-

-ro- ra que i- lus- tra el za- fir, al ver u- na au- ro- ra que i- lu- stra el za- fir, ar- ded y _

_ lu- cid, [ar- ded _ y _ lu- cid, ar- ded y _ lu- cid.]

Fine

attacca

Coplas

1. Las flo- res del cie- lo _ ar- dan; los as- tros del cam- po _ bri- llen;
2. Las ro- sas sus ra- yos _ co- pien; los or- bes sus lu- ces _ pin- ten;
3. La es- tre- lla a sus o- jos _ mue- re; el al- ba al va- lien- te _ vi- ve;
4. Lu- ce- ros su plan- ta _ hue- lla; cla- ve- les su vis- ta _ ti- ñe;
5. Ti- nie- blas in- tac- ta _ ven- ce; re- fle- jos con- stan- te _ ci- ñe;
6. Los pe- chos a- man- te _ hie- re; las al- mas pia- do- sa _ ri- je;

D.C. Estribillo

les, las flo- - res ar- dan, los as- tros bri- llen.
les, las ro- - sas co- pien, los or- bes bri- ten.
ces, la es- tre- - lla mue- re, el al- ba vi- ve.
ces, lu- ce- - ros hue- lla, cla- ve- les ti- ñe.
bles, ti- nie- - blas ven- ce, re- fle- jos ci- ñe.
ve, los pe- - chos hie- re, las al- mas ri- je.

[15] Al Santísimo Sacramento

Juan Hidalgo

Coplas

1. A- ves__ que al sol__ des- per- táis___ de su__ cu- na de cla-
2. Quie- ro__ bien a u- na a- zu- ce- na; en- tre__ ca- ra can- di-
3. Quie- ro__ bien a a- quel ma- ná___ que pre- ser- va- do se__
4. Quie- ro__ bien a a- quel za- gal, __ que no__ le per- mi- to__

-vel,   a- mad   y   sa- bed   de __ mí   que quie-   ro has- ta __ no   sa-
-dez,   sien- to   mis   o-   jos   he-   lar- se   y   mi   co-   ra- zón   sa ar- del __
ve   de las   in-   jus- ti-   cias   del __   tiem-   po con de-   sa-   gra- mis   o   vio del __
ser   de los   o-   jos __   mí-   os __   cuan-   do ga- lán   de   mis __ o-   jos __

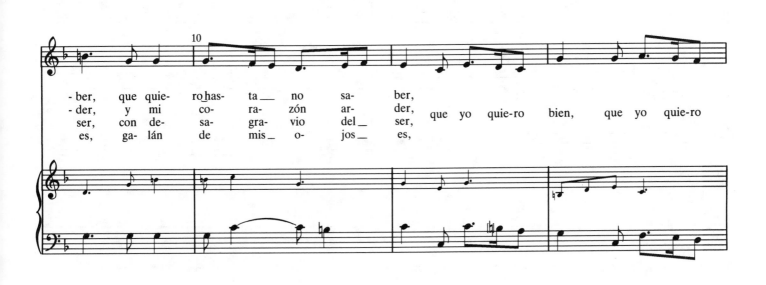

-ber,   que quie-   ro has- ta __   no   sa- ber,
-der,   y   mi   co-   ra- zón   ar- der,   que   yo   quie-ro   bien,   que   yo   quie-ro
ser,   con de-   sa-   gra- vio   del __   ser,
es,   ga- lán   de   mis __ o-   jos __   es,

bien   a a- quel que me   quie- re sin dar- le a en- ten- der   que yo quie-ro,   yo quie-ro,   yo quie-ro   bien.

[16] Tono humano

Estribillo

Juan Hidalgo

Vi- va mi es- pe-ran- za pues que lle-go a ver la dei-dad de Fi- lis,

que al-gún dí- a fue in- gra-ta ti- ra- na, más be-nig-na, y pues mi gran-de for-tu- na

pu-do me-re- cer de Fi- lis fa-vo- res, pu- bli-que mi fe; vi- va mi es-pe-ran- za

pues ya lle-go a ver que en Fi- lis no hay ri- gor ni des-dén.

Fine

attacca

Coplas

1. Dul- cí- si- mo due- ño mí- o, per- do- na si te_a-
2. Con tus lu- ce- ros a- lum- bras to- da_un al-ma_a que____
3. So- la tú, due- ño que- ri- do, me_has cau- ti- va- do;____

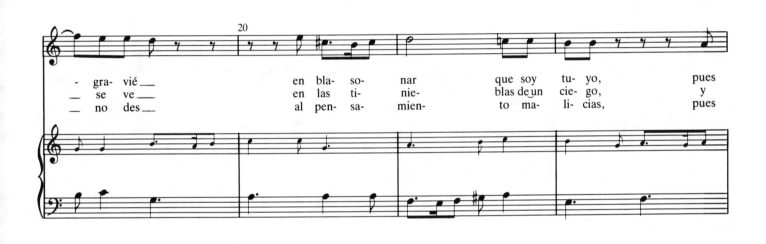

- gra- vié____ en bla- so- nar que soy tu- yo, pues
_ se ve____ en las ti- nie- blas de_un cie- go, y
_ no des____ al pen- sa- mien- to ma- li- cias, pues

D.C. Estribillo

mi_es- pe- ran-za_ha de ser ser- vir pa- ra_a- mar____ pos- tra-do_a tus pies.____
pues me_en- se- ño_a que- rer: vi- va mi_es- pe- ran- za por sig- los, a- mén.____
ves que no pue- de ser, pues só- lo tú so- la mi due-ño_has de ser.____

[17] Tonada a San Francisco

Juan del Vado

La más pu-ra a-zu- ce- na su a- fec- to en-no- ble- ció por pre-ser-var- le

Violón

Arpa

siem- pre el in-tac- to can- dor, por- que___ no tie- nen im- pre-sio-

- nes de som- bras tu cán-di- do ful- gor, im-pre-sio- nes de som- bras tu cán-di- do ful- gor.

[18] Solo y acompañamiento

Anonymous

Con a- man- tes in- - quie- tu- des, Te- re- sa, de sua- ve in- cen- dio, in- cen- dio, sur- ca, ven- ce, lo- gra, bus- ca, ma- res, vi- cios, triun- fos, puer- tos: sur- ca ma- res, ven- ce vi- cios, lo- gra triun- fos, bus- ca puer- tos.

[19] Solo al Santísimo

Si en- tre flo- res her- mo- sas ás- pi- des an- dan y la vi- da cau-ti- van con lo que ha- la- gan, ¡flo- res al ar- ma!, ¡fuen- tes al ar- ma!, ¡a- ves al ar- ma! An- de a- ler- ta el cui- da- do por la cam- pa- ña. Flo- res, fuen- tes, a- ves, ¡al

ar-ma, al ar- ma! An-de a-ler- ta el cui- da- do por ___ la ___ cam- pa- ña.

Coplas

1. For- men fren- te de ban- de- ras los jaz- mi- nes en hi- le- ras al pu- ro cla-
2. La pre- cio- sa ar- ti- lle- rí- a ha- ga her- mo- sa ba- te- rí- a en per- las que
3. El pe- li- ca- no a- mo- ro- so se a el sac- re ge- ne- ro- so que al a- ve noc-
4. Es- te tu- li- pán ne- va- do de real púr- pu- ra lis- ta- do des- cu- bra cual
5. Fo- sos se- an de cris- ta- les cuan- tos vier- ta en ma- nan- tia- les la vis- ta que al
6. Ni- do po- bre al fé- nix de o- ro de mi pe- cho con- de- co- ro, for- man- do ar- dor

- vel triun- fan- te, sol ra- dian- te que en la nie- ve os- ten- ta lla- mas.
se de- rra- man y se in- fla- man en la ho- gue- ra que a- mor fra- gua.
- tur- na y fie- ra en su ho- gue- ra siem- pre ten- ga a pri- sio- na- da.
cen- ti- ne- la la cau- te- la que en el cam- po se de- rra- ma.
sol en- tre- ga lin- ce y cie- ga de la fe di- cho- sa es- cla- va.
su des- ve- lo de mi hie- lo cuan- do le a- cuar- te- la el al- ma.

¡Flo- res, al ar- ma, al ar- ma, flo- res, al ar- ma, al ar- ma!
¡Fuen- tes, al ar- ma, al ar- ma, fuen- tes, al ar- ma, al ar- ma!
¡A- ves, al ar- ma, al ar- ma, a- ves, al ar- ma, al ar- ma!
¡Flo- res, al ar- ma, al ar- ma, flo- res, al ar- ma, al ar- ma!
¡Fuen- tes, al ar- ma, al ar- ma, fuen- tes, al ar- ma, al ar- ma!
¡A- ves, al ar- ma, al ar- ma, a- ves, al ar- ma al ar- ma!

[20] Solo al Santísimo Sacramento

[Juan de] Navas

-vi- no a- mor, [ay,] _____ di- vi- no a- mor, ay, _____ a- mor, que

fluc- tuan- do _____ ma- res, ma- res, ré- mo-ra de ti

mis- mo, mis- mo, ré- mo-ra de ti mis- mo, mis- mo,

se- gu- ro ___ puer- to _____ ha- llas- te. A tu o- be-

-dien- cia siem-pre te rin-dan va- sa- lla- je los pra-dos y las sel- vas, los mon-tes y los

va- lles, a tu o- be- dien- cia siem- pre te rin- dan va- sa- lla- je

los pra- dos y las sel- vas, los mon-tes y los va- lles.

Coplas

1. Dei- dad por lo en- cen- di- do, en- [cen- di- do] de sus ac- ti-
2. Aun más de lo im- po- si- ble, im- [po- si- ble] hoy en tu pe-
3. De un pe- cho e- na- mo- ra- do, e- na- [mo- ra- do] ven- ces di- fi-
4. Al vien- to da las ve- las, las ____ [ve- las] de tus fe- li-
5. De- cir- le que bien quie- ra, bien ____ [quie- ra] muy bien pue- des
6. Na- ve- ga vien- to en po- pa, en ____ [po- pa,] pues e- res hoy ___

-vi- da- des, _
-cho ha- llas- te, _
-cul- ta- des; _
-ci- da- des, _
-cu- sar- se, _
_ la _ na- ve _

se a- bra- sa ma- ri- po- - sa, ma- ri- po-
si de an- ti- guas ce- ni- - zas, ce- ni-
fue siem- pre a- tre- vi- mien- - to, a- tre- vi- mien-
pues ya en su cen- tro vi- - ve, vi-
si a- mán- do- se a sí mis- - mo, a sí mis-
fiel de- se- a- do puer- - to, puer-

2 6 7 6

D.C. Estribillo

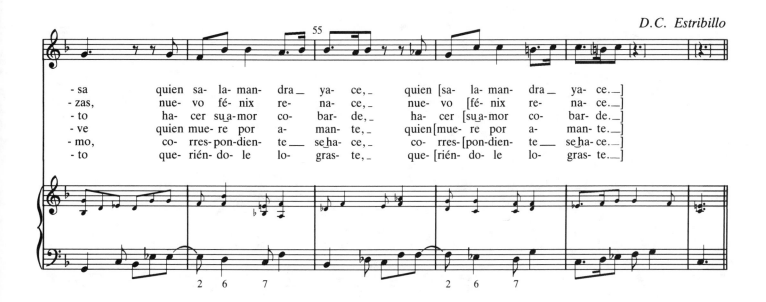

- sa
- zas,
- to
- ve
- mo,
- to

quien sa- la- man- dra _ ya- ce, _
nue- vo fé- nix re- na- ce, _
ha- cer su a- mor co- bar- de, _
quien mue- re por a- man- te, _
co- rres- pon- dien- te _ se ha- ce, _
que- rién- do- le lo- gras- te, _

quien [sa- la- man- dra _ ya- ce.]
nue- vo [fé- nix re- na- ce.]
ha- cer [su a- mor co- bar- de.]
quien [mue- re por a- man- te.]
co- rres- [pon- dien- te _ se ha- ce.]
que- [rién- do- le lo- gras- te.]

2 6 7 2 6 7

[21] Tono humano

Estribillo

[Juan de] Navas

Pues- to que ba- ja el a- mor a _ la _ tie- rra de cán- di- dos

cis- nes ba- tien- do las a- las, su- dan- do el ca-

-lor que [en] el pe- cho se en- cien- de des- hi- len los o- jos o- cé- a- nos de a- gua.

Fine

attacca

Coplas

1. Pues hoy la for- tu- na se su- be a su es- fe- ra, que son los
2. A he- rir de E- ri- tre- a y de Cin- tia los pe- chos la he- bra flo-
3. Al ai- re me su- bo a en- cen- der un pe- li- gro por- que los

va- gos pa- la- cios del vien- to, des- pues pe- pa- ra ha-
-ri- da fe- cun- da mi plan- ta, pues pa- ra ha-
hom- bres, e- rra- dos al ver- lo, por cas- ti- go lo

-di- das las lla- mas del al- ma, llo- ren los o- jos cen- te- llas de fue- go.
-cer- los en to- do in- fe- li- ces ha- cer que- ri- dos los jó- ve- nes bas- ta.
ten- gan y no por des- di- cha y mi en-vi- dia pa- rez- ca in- flu- jo del cie- lo.

[22] Solo humano

Estribillo   Anonymous

Ni- ña, si en-con- tra- res dur- mien- do a Cu- pi- do,   si ve- lar no

quie- res, dé- ja- le, dé- ja- le, [dé- ja- le, dé- ja- le] dor- mi- do.

Coplas

1. Dur- mien-do es- ta- ba u-na tar- de en las flo- res Cu- pi-

-di- llo, que se duer- me fá- cil- men- te quien es cie- go y quien _____ es ni- ño.

2. No_es- tá siem- pre_A- - mor des- pier- to; tal vez sue- le con- du-

-cir- lo la mu- dan- za y_el can- san- cio al le- tar- go del _____ ol- vi- do.

3. Y_u- na za- ga- le- ja li- bre de su_a- mo- ro- so do-

-mi- nio no que- rien- do que- rer nun- ca qui- so des- per- tar- le _____ y qui- so.

[23] Tonada sola con flautas para contralto

Contralto

Estribillo

Sebastián Durón

Flute*

Co- ra-zón, cau- - sa_te- néis, si sen-tís, si sus- - pi- ráis,

si tem- bláis,_____ si pa- de- céis, pues el Dios a quien te-

-méis es el que_in- jus- to_a- gra-váis, y_es- tre- cha cuen- ta____ da- réis._____

*The title gives plural for flute, but only one flute part is known.

Co- ra- zón, cau- sa__ te-

- néis, si sen- tís, si sus- pi- ráis, si tem- bláis,_____ si tem- bláis,_____

eco

si____ pa- de- céis, si_____ pa- de- céis._____

Coplas

1. Si te- méis la es- tre- cha cuen- ta del se- ve- rí- si- mo juez,
2. Si pa- de- céis sus pe- sa- res, el me- dio más dig- no es,
3. El ver- le cru- ci- fi- ca- do os ha- ga llo- rar por ver
4. Si sen- tís el pro- pio e- rror, _____ sen- tís, co- ra- zón, muy bien,

más del ca- so es en- men- dar que gas- tar tiem- po en te- mer.
de- sen- ga- ñán- doos del mun- do, cru- ci- fi- ca- ros con él.
quan mal vues- tra in- gra- ti- tud pa- ga tan cons- tan- te fe.
y se- rá e- ter- no vi- vir mo- men- tá- neo pa- de- cer.

Si llo- ráis

y pa- de- céis, co- ra- zón, cau- sa te- néis, cau- sa te- néis,

cau- - sa__ te- néis, cau- - sa te- néis._____

[24] Tonada humana

Sebastián Durón

1. Pues me pier- do_en lo que ca- llo el des- dén de
2. Dí- la, que no_es- toy en mí_____ de lo- grar tu

lo que_a- do- ro,__ ¡gran bo-be- rí- a, ca- pri- cho lo-
des- dén so- lo.__ ¡Gran bo-be- rí- a, ca- pri- cho lo-

- co   fue- ra   por ser ca- lla- do   no ser di- cho-   so!
- co   fue-ra̲ha- ber- me que- da- do   con- mi- go pro-   pio!

¿Gus- tas?   Ya soy dis- cre- to, pues no soy cor- to.   ¿Te̲e- no-   jas?

Pues, no quie- ro.   Vuel- vo̲a ser bo- bo, vuel- vo̲a ser bo- bo.

[25] Cantada a voz sola al Santísimo y de Pasión

Recitado

[Sebastián] Durón

Ay de mí, que el llan-to y la tris-te- za no, no ab- lan- da mi du- re-

-za. Cri- ad, Se- ñor, en mí pie-dad, u- san- do ____ un

lim- pio co- ra- zón, hu- mil- de y blan- do, y pa- ra que res- pi- ren mis sen-

-ti- dos, dad go- zo y a- le- grí- a a ____ mis o- í- dos.

Aria

1. Con- si- ga a-fli- gi- do mi a-fec- to ren- di- do la gra- cia __ que el
2. Aun- que soy in- dig- no, tu ros- tro be- nig- no, mi due- ño, __ no a-

al- ma in- fe- li- ce per- dió— a- fli- gi- do, ren- di- do, la
-par- tes __ de mi co- ra- zón; tu __ ros- tro be- nig- no, mi

gra- cia __ que el al- ma in- fe- li- ce per- dió, la gra- cia __ que el
ño, __ no a- par- tes __ de mi co- ra- zón, mi due- ño, __ no a-

al- ma in- fe- li- ce per- dió— pues nun- ca el que
-par- tes __ de mi __ co- ra- zón; ni qui- tes ai-

lle- ga llo- ran- do y se en- tre- ga con el tri- to y hu- mil- de des-
-ra- do tu es- pí- ri- tú a- ma- do, del al- ma a- fli- gi- da que

48

-pre- cia mi Dios, con- tri- to y hu- mil- de des- pre- cia mi Dios.

pi- de per- dón, del al- ma a- fli- gi- da que pi- de per- dón.

Recitado

Mas, ¡ay!, que aun-que el do- lor mi a- lien- to ex- ce- de, na- die el per- dón a- se- gu-

-rar- me pue- de, pues sa- bien- do la cau- sa por-que llo- ro, si es- tá bo- rra- do

mi de- li- to ig- no- ro, y co- mo te- me- ro- sa- men- te es-

-pe- ro, con te- mor y es- pe- ran- za vi- vo y mue- ro.

[26] Cantada al Santísimo con violines

-bra- so de_a-mor en la lla- ma! ¡Qué dul- ce vio- len- cia!

¡Qué tier- na re- ga- la! ¡Qué dul- ce, qué tier- na re-ga-

- la!

Ce-les- tes in- cen-dios al pe- cho mo- ti-van, que an-he-la el tor-

- men-to, que es glo-ria del al- ma.   ¡Ay, que me a-bra- so!   [¡Ay, que me a-

-bra- so] de a- mor en la lla- ma! [¡Ay, que me a-

-bra- so de a- mor en la lla- ma!] ¡Qué dul- ce

re- ga- la!   ¡Qué tier- na re- ga-

- la!

¡Qué tier- na re- ga- la!

Recitado

O gue- rra mis- te- rio- sa en la for- ma glo- rio- sa, vi- va-

-men- te con- tem- plo a quien e- ri- ge tem- plo, an-

[Fine]

-sio-sa el al- ma mí-   a,   re- me- dio de mi   cie-   ga fan- ta- sí-   -   a.

Aria

No de- je de_ar- der mi fiel co- ra- zón; se- rá la_o- ca-

-sión__ de mi me- re- cer— no, no, no

58

no,_____ no, no___ de- je de ar- der; no, no, no,___ no,___

no,_____ no, no de- je de ar- der; ve- rá_____ que_en su fue- go la

60

Coplas

1. A- ni- me a- mor, la__ lla- ma del ce- les- tial in- cen- dio, se- ré en sus pu- ras__
2. A- vi- ve la ma- te- ria mi a- mor y mi de- se- o, pres- tan- do mis sus-
3. El co- ra- zón la o- fren- da se- rá, pues el pri- me- ro fue quien al due- ño__

a- las glo- rio- so_ fé- nix_ si re- naz- co al_ cie- lo.
-pi- ros al ai- re_ que vo- raz a- ni- ma el_ fue- go.
mí- o fran- queó las_ puer- tas_ del hu- ma- no_ tem- plo.

Grave

Y en tan ce- les- tia- les di- vi- nos in- cen-dios, al sua- - ve_a-mo- ro- so sus- - pi- ro que_ex-

[D.C. Estribillo]

- ha- la, re- pi- - ta mi pe- cho su fiel con- so- nan- cia.

[27] Solo humano

Estribillo

[Juan de Lima] Serqueira

Que- rí- a Cu- pi- do, trai- dor y ha-la- güe- ño, he- rir con sus fle- chas de A-

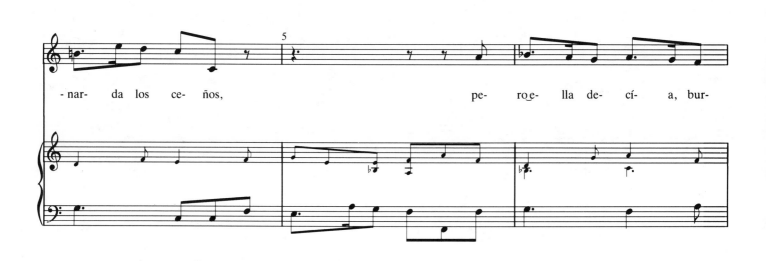

-nar- da los ce- ños, pe- ro e- lla de- cí- a, bur-

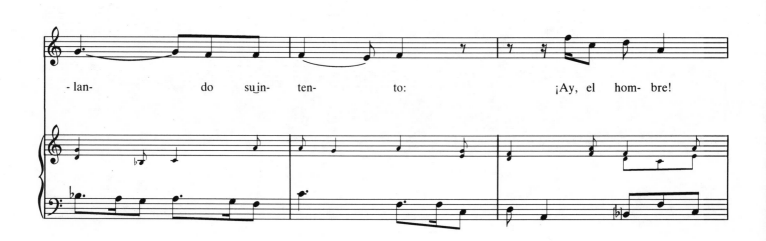

-lan- do su in- ten- to: ¡Ay, el hom- bre!

¡Ay, qué ho-rror! ¡Ay, qué mie- do! Ren- dir mi du- re- za.

¡Na- da me- nos que e- so! ¡Na- [da me- nos que e- so!]

Coplas

1. Que- rí- a el ti- ra- no ra- paz, ce- gue- zue- lo, que en mí la bel- dad, que na-
2. Que- rí- a en mis o- jos, mi- ran- do el in- cen- dio que a la i- ra so- pla el vol-
3. Que- rí- a que al ma- yo fér- til de mi ce- ño (le u- sur- pé e el ver- dor) la trai-
4. Que- rrá al fin que___ de mi es- tra- go mes- mo na- cie- se el que- dar- le la

- ció a ser he- chi- zo, pa- ra- se en ser ries- go.
- cán, me to- ca- sen las chis- pas del fue- go.
- ción de un in- flu- jo en- tra- se de e- ne- ro.   ¡Ay, el hom- bre!   ¡Ay, qué ho-rror! ¡Ay, qué
glo- ria del tiem- po y a mí el es- car- mien- to.

mie- do!

Ren- dir   mi   du-   re- za.
Que me ar- mé   yo   mis- ma.
Mar- chi- tan des-   de- nes.
Triun- far   de quien   rin- de.

¡Na-   da me-

- nos que e- so,   na- da me- nos que e-   so!

[28] Solo humano

[Juan de Lima] Serqueira

Estribillo

Ay, Leo-ni- da,   si mis que-jas,   mis sus- pi- ros   son li-son- jas de _

_tus ce- ños, de mis pe- nas son___ tes- ti- gos. El ai- re se

que- ja de ver- se o- pri- mi- do con el em- ba- ra- zo de tan- - tos ge- mi- dos.

Fine

attacca

Coplas

1. No ha- go car- go a tu be- lle- za de mi ro- ba- do al- be- drí-
2. Ya___ po- dré yo con- ten- tar- me con que tu des- dén es- qui-
3. Pár- ta- se en los dos el cos- te de es- te a- man- te sa- cri- fi-

D.C. Estribillo

- o, que no es cul- pa de tus o- jos el ha- ber- [me] yo per- di- do.
- vo; no mu- de el nom- bre es- ta o- fren- da y me la lla- me de- li- to.
- cio, y pues pon- go en el al- ma por ri- que- za lo be- nig- no.

[29] Tono humano solo

Estribillo

[Juan de Lima] Serqueira

To-do es a- mor: el a- rro- yo,   la es-tre- lla y la   flor;   a-

-pren- de, Tir- si be- lla,   de la flor,   el a- rro- yo

y la es-tre- lla, y   ve-   rás tu_____   ri-   gor; que na-da es des-

-dén; que to-do es a- mor: el a- rro- yo, la es- tre - lla, la flor,

y llo- ran - do, ar- dien- do, es- pi- ran - do,

en cris- tal, en in- cen - dio, en o- lor, el a- rro- yo, la es- tre

- lla y la flor; na - da es des- dén; to - do es a- mor: el a- rro-yo, llo-

-ran- do en cris- tal, en in- cen- dios ar- dien- do__ la es- tre- lla y la flor es- pi-

-ran- do en__ o- lor. To- do es a- mor: llo- ran- do el a- rro- yo, ar- dien- do la es- tre- lla es- pi-

-ran- do la flor, en cris- tal, en in- cen- dio en o- lor.

To- do es a- mor: el a- rro- yo, la es- tre- lla, la flor.

Fine

attacca

Coplas

1. A- quel a- rro- yue- lo, ga- lán de las sel- vas, sus tron- cos i-
2. Ra- yos es- par- cien- do, la a- mo- ro- sa es- tre- lla a vo- ces ar-
3. La flor ca- ri- ño- sa al sol ga- lan- te- a, ar- dien- do sus
4. A- ma, in- gra- ta Tir- si, pues a a- mor te in- vo- co, a- man- do el a-

-nun- da y sus flo- res rie pier-
-dien- tes la au- ro- ra des- pier-
ra- yos en di- cho- sa ho- gue-
-rro- yo, la flor y la es- tre-

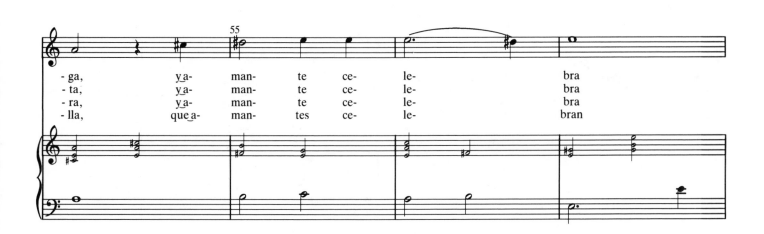

-ga, y a- man- te ce- le- le- bra
-ta, y a- man- te ce- le- le- bra
-ra, y a- man- te ce- le- le- bra
-lla, que a- man- tes ce- le- bran

con   llan-   to   de   cris-   tal   de a-   mor _____
con   e-   cos   de es- plen-   dor   de a-   mor _____
con   sus-   pi-   ros   de o-   lor   de a-   mor _____
en   cris-   tal, luz   y o-   lor   de a-   mor _____

las   pe-   nas,   con   llan- to   [de   cris- tal   de a-
las   pe-   nas,   con   e-   cos   [de es- plen- dor   de a-
las   pe-   nas,   con   sus-   [pi- ros   de o- lor   de a-
las   pe-   nas,   en   cris- tal, [luz y o-   lor   de a-

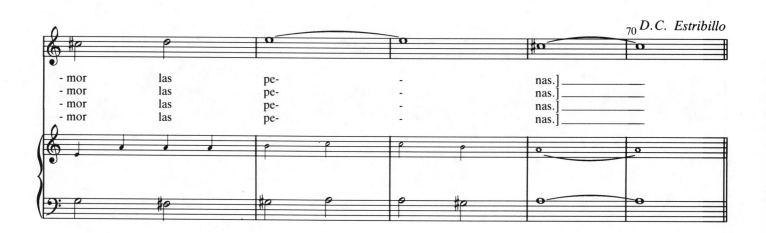

D.C. Estribillo

- mor   las   pe-   -   nas.] _____
- mor   las   pe-   -   nas.] _____
- mor   las   pe-   -   nas.] _____
- mor   las   pe-   -   nas.] _____

[30] Cantada humana

[Juan de Lima] Serqueira

*These instrumental parts have been reconstructed by the editor.

-man- te cuan-do fa- llez- - - co, fa- llez- co yo.

Recitado

Fi- li, si es- te sus- pi- ro, es- ta an- sia, __ es- ta fi- ne- za al- gu- na se- ña

de- ja a tu pie- dad fi- a- da, va- ya mi vi- da al ai- re en- co- men- da- da, mas, ¡ay!, que si mi

voz lle- va mi a- cen- to, el vien- to lle- va- rá lo que es del vien- to.

Aria

Ni tú

pue-des de- jar, Fi-li her- mo- sa, de ser ri- gu- ro- sa, in- gra- ta y cru- el.

Ni tú pue-des de- jar, Fi-li-her-mo- sa, de ser ri- gu- ro- sa, in- gra- ta y cru-

-el, de ser ri- gu- ro- sa, in gra- - - ta y cru- el.

[31] Cantada humana

Recitado

[Juan de Lima] Serqueira

En la ri- be- ra ver- de del pa- trio Man-za- na- res, a- sí Mar-ce- lo

Continuo*

can- ta a su a- do- ra- do bien que- jas a- man- tes.

Aria

Violin*

Oboe*

*These instrumental parts have been reconstructed by the editor.

mas no a- ca- be de ____ mo- rir.

Fine

No ____ por- que quie- ro vi- vir, si- no por más ___ pa- de- cer,

que muer- to po- dré que- rer pe- ro ____ no po- dré sen- tir.

[D.C. Aria al Fine]

Recitado

Be- li- sa, yo_obs-ti- na- do he de_a-do-rar- te, aun-que te pier- da_mi_in-fe- li- ce

suer- te, pues por el in- te-rés de no per- der- te, no_he de de-jar el mé-ri- to_de_a- mar- te. Pues si del des-

-ti- no la in-flü- en- cia me die-re por cas- ti- go el de_la_au- sen- cia, ad- vier- te que_al a-

-lien- to de_un sus- pi- ro no_hay se- gu- ra dis- tan- cia_en el re- ti- ro.

a- me fiel__ mi_____ co- ra- zón.

Que el a- lien- to por tor- men- to tan vio- len- to no es bien, de- je la pa- sión,

que el a- lien- to por tor- men- to tan vio- len- to no es bien, de- je la

pa- sión,
no es bien, de- je la pa- sión.

[D.C. Aria al Fine]

Fuga

A- guas que co- rréis,

-ti- vo de mi pa- de- cer, y el dul- ce tor- men- to de a- mor ex- pli-

-cad al___ be- llo mo- ti- vo de mi pa- de- cer, al be- llo mo-

-ti- vo de mi pa- de- cer.

Fine

matura sunt omnia